Murder Aboard
the
Queen Elizabeth II

Also by Stephen Murray

The Chapel of Eternal Love
Wedding Stories from Las Vegas
ISBN: 978-0-9911940-0-1
$14.95us

Return to the Chapel of Eternal Love
Marriage Stories from Las Vegas
ISBN: 978-0-9911940-1-8
$14.95us

Murder Aboard the Queen Elizabeth II

a novel by

Stephen Murray

Copyright © 2017 by Stephen Murray
ISBN 978-0-9911940-2-5
$14.95

Printed in the United States of America

www.murderaboardtheqe2.com

Cover design by Cynthia Carbajal

DEDICATIONS

For Pauline Gelavis
and
Kolleen Voigt

ACKNOWLEDGMENTS

To my family and friends — RJ, Sue, Grayham, Maria and Kolleen for all their support and encouragement.

To my writers group — Sue, Gail, Deborah, Nancy and Donelle for all their invaluable advice and suggestions throughout the process.

To Barbara Beckley for all her help with editing and for making the process a joy.

To members of the Atria Sunlake Book Club – Arla, Clarita, Creal, Frank, Ida, Jeanne, Joan, June, Marion, Melody, Pam, Shirley and Valerie.

Special thanks to James Kelly, Aspects of Writing, Inc. and Brian Rouff and staff, Imagine Communications of Henderson, Nevada.

CHAPTER 1

Sylvia Sinclair was admiring the beautiful terraced gardens of her Beverly Hills estate from the drawing room window. Twilight was always her favorite time of day. It was a balmy spring Southern California evening, and the setting sun created a deep crimson hue over the mountains behind the Los Angeles skyline. A smattering of snow on a few of the mountains created a majestic panorama. She watched the palm trees at the edge of her front garden swaying slowly in the soft, gentle breeze and sat quietly, sipping her sherry. Despite having lived in America for most of her life, the traditions she inherited from her British upper class upbringing were still very much a part of her.

Sylvia watched her husband's Jaguar turn slowly into the driveway and make its way up the slight incline. Within minutes, he came into the drawing room and greeted her with his customary light kiss on the cheek.

"And how was your day, honey?" he asked routinely, as he poured himself a glass of scotch from the crystal decanter.

He was still struck by her beauty and how she managed to keep her appearance so youthful. Her still natural shoulder length blond hair curled around her perfectly complexioned face belied the fact she would shortly be celebrating her fifty-first birthday.

"Much of it was spent composing and writing the

guest invitations for our silver wedding anniversary celebration."

"I don't know why you don't have them pre-printed and sent. It's so much easier."

"I enjoy writing them, darling. Besides, I think it is just good etiquette. The pre-printed ones are so impersonal. It's not as if there are that many to write anyway. After all, we are only inviting our family and our closest friends."

"Are you sure this is how you want to celebrate this occasion? A cruise on the Queen Elizabeth?"

"It's the perfect way to celebrate! Just think of it, darling — flying to London, spending a few days shopping, then cruising back from Southampton to New York. During August, we should have wonderful weather. Besides, the sea air will do you a world of good. It should help your blood pressure."

"I don't know. Somehow I just don't have a good feeling about it," he said ominously, and with atypical prescience. "But then, whatever makes you happy, my dear." He kissed her again.

She looked at him. Brian was as handsome as when she first met him in the early sixties. Now middle-aged, his rugged face and determined jaw line was tan and bronzed. His muscular physique was still evident from regular tennis playing and workouts at the gym. The once jet-black hair had turned prematurely silver, yet made his appearance more distinguished.

When they first met, his fledgling record production company, Sinclair Records, was in its infancy and, along with his business partner, Greg Calderman, he was struggling, but determined to succeed. Sylvia remembered auditioning for him as a singer, and although she made a few records, somehow the singing career she dreamed of never materialized. A year later, the Beatles stormed America and paved the way for what became known as the British Invasion. Brian had an uncanny knack for spotting musical talent and marketing it, and was able to capitalize on a host of British singers and rock groups. His company soared to success. Greg handled all the financial investments with wizardry, and the two men soon presided over a multimillion dollar empire.

Unfortunately, Brian uncovered an extensive web of deceit Greg had masterminded, siphoning off some of the profits and diverting them to Swiss bank accounts. Greg vehemently denied the accusations and insisted someone had set him up as the fall guy. But Brian felt he had the necessary proof and turned the evidence over to the District Attorney. The threat of a public scandal and humiliation caused Greg to take his own life before the case came to court. Out of respect for Greg's wife, Terri, Brian dropped the charges, but his bitterness and sense of betrayal stayed with him. Terri left for Europe shortly after Greg's death, convinced of her husband's innocence, but without the financial resources to sue Brian's empire.

Sylvia pondered her husband's last statement. *Whatever makes me happy, indeed,* she lamented. She still loved him. Even though the nagging rumors about his constant infidelity bothered her, Sylvia never found the courage to confront him, unsure of where the discussion might lead. The last thing she wanted was a divorce which, for her, was out of the question. She would not endure the public embarrassment, and her breeding dictated she maintain a stiff upper lip. Besides, she was still attracted to him. He had always been a good provider — she lacked for nothing — and had been a decent father to their two children, Robin and Stephanie. It pained her, though, that Stephanie and her father hadn't spoken for more than two years. She'd done everything possible to heal the wounds, but Stephanie had inherited her father's strong willed temperament and stubbornness. The relationship between the two had always been stormy.

"He'll never amount to anything!" Brian warned Stephanie when she asked him for help to set up an art gallery for her soon-to-be husband.

"Dad, it's not as if we are asking you to give us the money. We're only asking for a loan. Jean-Louis is a very gifted artist. He's going to be a phenomenal success. I just know it," she pleaded.

"What he paints is not art. It's abstract rubbish. Besides, he's no good for you. You better not have any plans of marrying this guy."

"I'm going to marry him anyway, whether you like it or not. And we'll get the gallery with your help or without it."

"Then you are on your own. Don't expect me to walk you down the aisle on your wedding day."

Defiantly, Stephanie and Jean-Louis eloped, and rented a small gallery on the outskirts of the artistic vortex of Sedona, Arizona. Jean-Louis was a temperamental, moody young Frenchman who was not intimidated by Brian's aggressive business demeanor. He felt uncomfortable around his father-in-law — it irked him when Stephanie's father tried to control her and he was tired of Brian's constant threats to exclude Stephanie from his will. Jean-Louis was happy when he and Stephanie moved away from her family, and his creativity flourished as a result. They made a fair living. It did not provide for the rich and privileged lifestyle Stephanie had known all her life, but she loved Sedona and discovered a talent of her own, making quality jewelry, which she marketed in various stores and boutiques throughout the town. She had not spoken to her father since she left Beverly Hills, which suited Jean-Louis. *The less contact with her family the better*, he thought. He was overly protective of Stephanie, some would say possessive, and was happiest when he received her full and undivided attention, while discouraging the friendships she was forming with their neighbors.

Sylvia hoped Stephanie would put her mother's wishes ahead of her own when Stephanie received the invite to join them on the cruise. She prayed the cruise would provide the perfect venue for daughter and father to reconcile. *Maybe I could make more of an effort to welcome Jean-Louis to the family,* she thought. *Perhaps that would help ease the tension.*

Robin made no attempt to conceal his dislike for his sister. He thought her totally selfish. All her life she had put her own needs and desires first, never thinking of the impact her actions had on the family. She knew her father wanted her to be a part of the family business, and planned to groom her to head up the marketing department. But no, she wanted to go to France and study at the Sorbonne. She returned to America with a starving French artist, whom Robin, like his father, thought worthless. As the current marketing manager of Sinclair Records was close to retirement, Brian would have to find someone else outside the company — and the family. Robin thought Stephanie could at least play a part in the company business. Since she was not remotely interested, he did not see why she should benefit from the rewards, including the estate.

Besides, Robin was not about to cross his father. He knew which side his bread was buttered on, and entered into his father's business with enthusiasm at the earliest opportunity. He was tough and ruthless, and hoped the giant Sinclair Records would one day be his. He also believed his father's story about Greg and the embezzlement of the vast sums of money when the company became successful. Robin's field of expertise was finance, and he was determined to ensure that the wealth of the company was well protected. There would be no similar frauds committed under his watch.

Brian was proud of his son, his male heir, and had a blind spot when it came to his faults. That Robin decided to follow in the family business made Brian aware his empire was not being built in vain. He wished his relationship with his daughter was as great as that with his son.

Sylvia had an entirely different perspective. She was under no illusion as to Robin's many character flaws. She admired ambition, but not the blind ambition so apparent in her son. She knew he would stop at nothing to get what he wanted when he wanted it. She disapproved of his fast paced and wild partying lifestyle and wished forlornly he would settle down and start a family. She suspected he took some form of drugs but, as with Brian's infidelities, looked the other way. Facing reality was not her strong suit. *I wonder which one of Robin's undesirable girlfriends he'll see fit to accompany him on the cruise*, she thought as she addressed his invitation. While hoping for the best, she dreaded the inevitable. She cared for none of partners and saw few redeeming attributes in any of them.

The loyal maid, Helen, who had worked for Brian and Sylvia for fifteen years, entered the room and announced dinner was ready. The couple headed toward the dining room, Sylvia thinking of all the planning she would have to do in the next couple of months, on what would prove to be their ill-fated celebration aboard the Queen Elizabeth II.

CHAPTER 2

Brian pulled back Sylvia's chair allowing her to be seated before taking his own place at the other end of the antique mahogany dining table.

Sylvia had insisted there were always to be lit candles and fresh flowers on the table at dinner time. Their presence provided a calming influence which she certainly needed that evening as she explained the guests she intended to invite to join them on their cruise.

Helen brought the bowls of vichyssoise to the table and poured a glass of wine for each of them.

"Well *of course* we'll have to invite the children and their partners," Sylvia said matter of fact, in response to Brian's suggestion to exclude them.

"I don't see why. Stephanie hasn't spoken to me for two years. I have nothing to discuss with whatever her husband's name is. You claim not to have anything in common with Robin's girlfriends. Why invite any of them?" he shrugged.

"You're absolutely right. I don't have anything in common with Robin's girlfriends. Probably because they are — well — common! But I will make every effort to be pleasant to Robin's guest, whoever she is, and it is high time you squared away your relationship with Stephanie and Jean-Louis. After all, this is our anniversary, and partially a family affair. Robin and Stephanie are the only family we have. It is right and proper we invite them."

Brian looked at his wife. He knew better than to pursue this line of discussion with her. Sylvia was a stickler for manners and doing the right thing, and would never entertain the notion of leaving either of the children out of their silver anniversary celebration. Brian had always left the social aspect of their marriage to her, and would not change now. It was an area of their life where Sylvia excelled.

"Well, who else are you inviting?" he continued.

"Marina and Todd."

Brian groaned.

"Marina is my best friend, and was my bridesmaid at our wedding. Surely you didn't think for a minute I would not invite her?"

Marina and Sylvia were childhood friends and neighbors. Marina was every bit as English as Sylvia, and from an equally well-to-do family. With her face covered in freckles, Marina knew she was not the most beautiful girl on the planet, but was still pretty in her own way. She was also fun-loving, sincere, down-to-earth and, above all, she worshiped Todd. As Sylvia was so quiet and reserved, she always admired Marina's gregarious and perky personality.

"Of course not. Marina is terrific. I've always liked her. It's Todd I object to."

Todd was advancing into his middle aged years and time had not been kind to him. Once a handsome young man with an adoring female following, he was now unable to control his weight, and the years of drinking showed heavily on his bloated face. His star as a recording artist had faded considerably.

"Perhaps you've forgotten I was bridesmaid at Marina's wedding and you were best man for Todd?" Sylvia reminded Brian drily.

"Only because he asked me. I did it more as a favor to Marina. I just believe he's a real pain. I always have."

"Well you shouldn't. He was one of your biggest recording stars ever. Sinclair Records has made their fortune from him alone."

Helen removed the empty soup bowls and served the main entrée. Brian relished the venison that lay before him accompanied by roasted potatoes and steamed asparagus. It was one of his favorite meals. He rose and poured Sylvia another glass of wine, and filled his own glass before returning to his seat.

"*Was!*,dear. *Was!* But not any longer," he continued. "Todd Hammond hasn't had a hit record in years. His voice is gone. I can't even get him a weekend gig at a Las Vegas lounge show. Worst of the matter is his contract is coming up shortly."

"You'll renew it of course," Sylvia interjected.

"I have absolutely no intention of renewing it. Biggest mistake we ever made was to sign him for a multi-year contract. So, if they accept the invitation, I hope he doesn't spend the entire time on the trip trying to discuss his demands. I don't want to have to break the news to him until we get back."

"I'm sure you'll handle it. It would be unthinkable not to include them — especially Marina. I have also invited the Claytons. Since Dave Clayton is your top recording artist and number one star, surely you can't object to my inviting him and Laura?"

"Oh, great," Brian retorted, dropping his knife and fork alongside his plate, folding his arms petulantly. "Now I have my former and current top stars at the same table at the same time. How do we all handle that?"

"Stop being silly, dear. You're making such a mountain out of a molehill. We're all adults. Todd and Dave might have egos, but the rest of us don't. It's our anniversary, and we should have those with us who have been closest over the years. Even Todd and Dave will respect that."

Dave and Laura were considered a glamour couple even though Dave was extremely conceited. But then he had just cause. He was a strikingly handsome man, with a mane of blond hair, tanned face, and piercing blue eyes. Approaching his mid-forties, he had a singing voice still admired and adored by millions of fans of both sexes. Laura was a former model who had maintained her svelte figure. She was almost famous in her own right, before sacrificing her career to be with him. She appeared to be his number one devoted fan, was always at his side, and joyously shared the limelight Dave's fame and fortune had brought them. Dave had everything working in his favor.

"The last person I've invited is Marshall," Sylvia concluded.

Brian was pleased about that. Marshall Thornton was the attorney for Sinclair Records in charge of all the contracts, and Brian's best friend. They had known each other since college days, and Marshall was best man at their wedding. It was also Marshall whom Brian had to thank for discovering the embezzlement of his business by Greg Calderman all those years ago.

Marshall was still quite suave. He had never married.

It was widely rumored he was a womanizer, but he never brought any female companions to any parties or functions, nor did he discuss any of his female friends. He always conversed and danced with unaccompanied ladies at all the events. He was a charming 'bon vivant' and Sylvia always enjoyed having him attend her parties when she invited single ladies.

"So there'll be eleven of us?"

"Well, I was wondering if I should round out the numbers by asking Alicia, since we all played Bridge together for so many years. But it may be a little too soon after Bruce's death. I also wouldn't want her to think we were matchmaking her with Marshall."

Alicia was an attractive female in her early fifties. Her husband, Bruce, was considerably older and had died a few months earlier from a sudden heart attack. They first met Brian on the tennis court. Although they still played together periodically, it was less frequent since Bruce passed. Brian missed playing across the court from her, as much as he missed their Bridge evenings. She was a good match for him at both pastimes.

Brian laughed. "Well, there have been worse mismatches. Personally, I think Alicia might welcome the change and to be among friends. It is not as if she doesn't know who Marshall is. We've had enough parties over the years so they're not exactly strangers. Besides, I could see them on the dance floor together. They both seem to enjoy dancing. Why don't you go ahead and invite her?"

The conversation was interrupted by the ringing telephone.

Brian dropped his napkin on the table and moved

toward the drawing room to answer it. Sylvia followed him with her cup of coffee in hand and sat pensively at her desk.

From the one-sided part of the telephone conversation she could hear, she knew Brian was talking to the producer of the hit television talent show, "America Sings".

Brian hung up the phone.

"Honey, they want me to be a panelist on tomorrow night's show. One of the regulars has come down with the flu'. You're welcome to come to the studio if you like."

"No thanks" she replied in a non-committal tone.

"Well, I think I'll watch the Dodger game on the TV in the family room."

"Don't forget to take your blood pressure pill," she shouted after him as she picked up her pen and started writing the invitation to Alicia.

CHAPTER 3

Denise Parker was ensconced in her favorite art deco chair with her feet tucked underneath, as she switched on her television using the remote control. Her glass of wine in hand, and a plate of *pate de foie gras* and crackers on the side table, it was time for her favorite weekly television show to start.

She always enjoyed watching 'America Sings' alone and in the comfort of her elegantly decorated Park Avenue penthouse in Manhattan. Her furnishings were tasteful, with very bright and vivid colors, reflecting her vibrant personality.

The theme tune of the show started and the host took center stage, bowing to the audience to thunderous applause as he did every week.

"Please give a warm welcome this evening to our special guest panelist," he intoned enthusiastically. "Many of you may not recognize his face, but you will all recognize his name. Please welcome famed record producer, agent to recording stars, and president of Sinclair Records, the multi-talented Brian Sinclair."

As the camera spun to Brian's face and zoomed for a close up, Brian smiled and nodded with fake coyness.

Denise took a large gulp from her wine glass. *He's more handsome and sexier than he ever was*, she thought. She had not seen him in years. Her mind drifted back, as it often did, recalling when she first became his fiancée, and how devastated she was when he broke off their engagement two years later in order to marry Sylvia. How she hated that woman. Brian had been the love of her life, and she had quietly carried a torch for him for over a quarter of a century — more than half her life. There had never been such a tender and passionate relationship before or since, and she had always been at a loss as to what attracted Brian to Sylvia. It certainly couldn't be her limited vocal talents. *Sure, Sylvia was an attractive woman, but a little cold and aloof,* Denise thought. Probably frigid, she imagined, and Denise knew how much Brian enjoyed his wild sex. Denise had never really cared for Sylvia. They were both rivals and competing for a contract with Sinclair records at the same time. Their paths often crossed at the studios as they mixed with the same circle of other would-be recording artists.

When Denise was engaged to Brian, it was her ambition to be a recording star, but he had never believed in her talent. After their separation, and upon learning of his almost immediate marriage plans to Sylvia, she was determined to seek her revenge, and show both of them she would make it. And she did. She sent a few sample discs to a rival record company. Her sultry, sensuous, sexy voice caught the ear of an executive, and she signed a contract. Fortunately, an aggressive and dynamic young manager was assigned to direct her career. Her first released record was a powerful love ballad that became a major international hit, and Denise Parker was on her way. A string of hit records through the sixties and seventies followed, after which, her career made its way into cabarets and concert appearances. Even though she no longer enjoyed recording chart status, the beautiful, petite, vivacious blond was still one of the most popular and sought after American female entertainers. It was one of the rare occasions when Brian had misjudged a talent. Denise often wondered if he had deliberately tried to sabotage her career. Is it possible she would have been more famous than he, and his masculine ego would not have been able to handle it? It was an opinion Denise and many of her friends had privately shared.

The TV host was making polite conversation with Brian on the show.

"And I hear you and your wife will soon be celebrating your silver wedding anniversary?"

The audience applauded loudly.

"Yes, as a matter of fact in August. We're taking the QEII from Southampton to New York to celebrate."

"Well, congratulations!" the host continued. "How wonderfully romantic!"

The audience applauded again.

Denise rapidly finished her wine and poured herself another glass. A few minutes later, she picked up the phone and dialed her agent.

"Leon, can you get me a gig on the QEII from Southampton to New York, the August departure?"

"Are you kidding me? They would never pay your fees. Besides you will have just completed your Canadian tour. You'll be exhausted." Yet, he was accustomed to her impulsive and impetuous ideas.

"So, the rest will be good for me. I don't care about the fee. If you have to, tell them I will do it for nothing."

"I'm sure they already have entertainment booked at this stage."

"Tell them to give me a guest star role. I don't want any advance publicity. I don't want anyone, least of all the public, to know about the cruise … and while you're at it, get me a first class suite."

"Denise, what's this all about? I don't get it."

"Leon, please for once will you just do something without giving me the third degree? Please, pretty please," she begged in a pouting tone.

"All right! All right! I'll see what I can do tomorrow." Leon hung up. He hated that mood. Of all his contract artists, Denise Parker was his most temperamental.

Denise watched the remainder of the show, but her mind was not focused on the talent this week. She was already planning her appearance on the QEII.

Across the country in California, Robin picked up the phone and dialed his latest girlfriend. "Pack your bags, babe! We're off on a cruise on the QEII." He threw himself back on his bed and loosened his tie.

"Say what? Are you teasing me? How's that going to happen?" Jill asked in disbelief.

"Didn't you watch 'America Sings' tonight? Dad told the nation. He and Mother are going on the QEII to celebrate their silver wedding anniversary."

"You never told me your dad was going to be on 'America Sings' tonight. But anyway, that doesn't mean we're invited. I've never even met your mom and dad."

Robin pondered Jill's last comment. He knew only too well his mother would never approve of Jill, since she never cared for of any of his girlfriends. Jill, who was brash and flashy, certainly would be no exception. Her tight faded jeans and skin tight blouses that accentuated her ample cleavage and revealed her heavily tattooed midriff would not be acceptable in Sylvia's world. Robin could almost visualize the disapproving look of his mother.

"Well, of course we're invited. Mother would never have a family affair and not invite her children. It's just not Mother. She always adds 'and guest' to my invitations. I'll guarantee the written invitation will arrive within a couple of days."

"Your mother still writes invitations? Is she for real?" quizzed Jill unbelievably.

"Yeah, that's Mother."

"Oh, I don't know. Maybe I won't fit in. Maybe it's not my scene."

"I want you with me, babe. You know I want you with me. Tell you what, I'll run you over to the house on Saturday afternoon. Mother and Dad are always at home then. Once you meet them, you'll feel better about it."

"Okay," she said slowly. "But make sure it happens this time. So often you've said you'd take me to meet your family. We've been dating for three months now, and every time you promise, you always back off at the last minute."

"Babe, are you going to start nagging me again? I call to invite you on a cruise — the QEII no less — and you start badgering me. What's with you? What's your problem?"

"I'm sorry honey. I didn't mean to ..."

Robin cut her off.

"I'll call you tomorrow." He slammed the phone down and headed to the bar where he grabbed the bottle of scotch in one hand and a tumbler in the other. He poured himself a stiff drink and flopped back on the couch in his living room. *Damn woman. You can never please a damn woman.*

He'd met his match with Jill, though. She was as devious and as calculating as he. She was playing her cards well, and she knew it. She knew she would soon be in the Sinclair family mansion.

"I'm home, honey," Brian yelled as he entered the house. Sylvia came down the stairs to join him in the living room. "Did you watch the show? What do you think? How did I do?"

"Did you have to broadcast to the entire world about our wedding anniversary plans?" she asked.

"What's the big deal?" Brian could tell she was annoyed.

"Why does our private life have to become public? Why does everyone have to know what we're doing? There will probably be all kinds of would-be-singers with grandiose ideas now traipsing around the QEII in the hopes of meeting you, all clamoring and fawning for an audition."

"Well that's good business for the QEII isn't it? All those extra passengers," he chuckled.

"I don't think this is at all amusing," said Sylvia huffily.

"Our family and guests haven't even received their invites yet. What must they be thinking if they hear our plans on the television?"

"I'm going to bed. I don't need this row about nothing. Not tonight. It's been a busy day. I thought I did a good job on the show tonight, and all you care about is your privacy and what is proper." Brian threw up his hands and prepared to leave.

"I'm sorry you think my thoughts and feelings are so unimportant," she retorted.

Brian left, slamming the heavily wooden living room door behind him and headed upstairs toward the bedroom.

Sylvia sat on the couch, fuming. Maybe she should just abandon the cruise, and make Brian look a complete idiot. But she was much too sensible to make decisions in anger. She would sleep on it, and decide the next morning. Much as she loved Brian, there were times when she wondered whether it was all worth it. She was getting tired of his casting her as the domesticated wife.

The clock on the wall said it was five minutes before nine. She called Marina.

"Marina, dear. How would you like to have dinner with me tomorrow evening?"

"Well, I'm available, but Todd isn't. He's giving an interview on some local radio station over the hill in the San Fernando Valley somewhere."

"That's fine. It can be girl's night out." She hoped it would be just the two of them. "Shall we say six-thirty at the Polo Lounge? I'll make reservations tomorrow morning."

"Great, I'll look forward to it."

They hung up. Sylvia was not ready to go to bed. She poured herself a glass of her favorite liqueur, Drambuie, and put on a long playing record keeping the volume low. Removing her shoes, she lay down on the couch listening to the soft, soothing and romantic sounds of Johnny Mathis. There was something to be said for solitude.

CHAPTER 4

Brian had already left for work when Sylvia woke up the next day. She decided to spend the morning gardening, always a relaxing and soothing pastime for her. Even though they employed a gardener, Sylvia enjoyed a little weeding, removing the dead petals from the roses, bougainvillea and the myriad of other assorted flowers in her colorful garden. It was a source of much pride.

She was still smarting from the events of the previous evening, not only from Brian announcing their plans for their anniversary on television, but also from his lack of understanding when she expressed her dismay. The garden helped brighten the day and put her in a better frame of mind.

At lunchtime, she savored a small snack of boursin cheese and crackers, before freshening up and leaving to have her hair done.

"Helen, I won't be home for dinner tonight. Just set the table for one," Sylvia called as she headed out the house toward the garage. She was not of the mind to explain her movements to Helen or why Brian would be dining alone that evening, knowing full well he would not be happy. If it was something Brian detested, it was eating alone. *It will serve him right* she thought as she sped along Sunset Boulevard toward the beauty salon.

For once, her hairdresser was on time and began creating his magic. Her hair was beautifully highlighted and coiffed as she drove up the palm tree lined entrance to the famed pink-colored Beverly Hills Hotel. Leaving her car with the valet, she headed toward the Polo Lounge. Marina was already there.

Sylvia made her way to where Marina was sitting, and was reminded of how her friend hadn't seemed to have changed over the years at all. Her slightly freckled and rosy cheeks were the same as they always had been, as had her curly hairstyle. Marina had always been relatively plain looking, but her effervescent, yet steadfast, personality made her an endearing friend — and very loyal wife.

"Oh, Sylvia," she gushed in delight as they hugged and kissed. "We received your invitation this afternoon. I tried calling. I am so excited. We'd be thrilled to join you."

"A sherry please — make that Harvey's Bristol Cream," Sylvia said to the cocktail waiter. Her friend was already sipping her usual martini. "I'm so glad you will be able to celebrate with us, Marina. It wouldn't be the same without you. Can you believe it's been twenty-five years?"

"I know. It's amazing. Who else is coming? Do tell," Marina encouraged excitedly.

"Well, the invitations only went out yesterday, so you are the first response. But, I'll fill you in on the guest list. You know them all, of course." Sylvia relayed the list of those to whom she had sent the invitations.

"I just know we'll have an awfully good time, Sylvia. It's just what Todd and I need right now. It'll be a breath of fresh air."

"Oh?" inquired Sylvia sensing something was amiss.

The cocktail waiter arrived with the sherry, and the

captain inquired as to their dining pleasure.

"Same as last week," Sylvia said.

"Make that two," Marina ordered indifferently as her mood became a little subdued. "To tell you the truth, Sylvia, it has been a real tough time these last few months. You know Todd hasn't had any hit records for quite a while. He can't seem to get any concert or television appearances anywhere. Tonight, he is on some crummy little local radio station over in the valley, which won't pay anything. The royalties we're receiving from his records are becoming less and less. You know what a reckless spender Todd is. He just can't economize. He wouldn't know how to begin. We're living way beyond our means."

"Marina, you're not saying you're having financial difficulties? That's impossible. Todd made a fortune from all those hit records."

"You can't breathe a word to anyone, Sylvia. Todd made some bad investments. I've tried talking with him, but he just goes into a fit of rage. He's impossible, and his drinking is getting worse. I'm half expecting them to foreclose on our home any day soon. Things are getting quite unbearable."

"Don't exaggerate, Marina. Surely it can't be that bad," Sylvia chided gently.

"I don't know. You know me, Sylvia — finances have never been my forte. I just have to surmise, and try and figure out where we stand from the little Todd tells me when he's had too much to drink which, unfortunately, is becoming more and more frequent."

"Don't worry. Something will turn up," Sylvia reassured.

"I'll just be glad when Brian renews Todd's contract at the end of August. That will relieve a lot of worry from Todd. Naturally, the regular monthly check we receive will help. Of course, since the last contract was signed years ago, we're sure Brian will compensate for inflation and rising costs over the years."

Sylvia, relieved the food arrived, deftly changed the subject to the beautifully prepared poached salmon that was placed in front of them both. She was not about to divulge Brian's sentiments on the subject of Todd's contract, even if Marina was her best friend. The thought reminded her that her husband was probably at home right now and having quite a tantrum. She was right.

At the house, Brian was piqued to find Sylvia not there, and not even know her whereabouts.

"Where the hell is she?" he demanded of Helen.

He was not about to dine alone and, after waiting for an hour, decided to eat out at a restaurant. At least there would be people around him. As he headed toward the garage, the sound of the telephone ringing stopped him.

"Hello!" he growled unwelcomingly.

"Well, that's a fine greeting from my second favorite man in the whole world," cooed Laura.

"Evening, my sweetheart," Brian demurred. His mood changed immediately. "You keep saying things like that, and I'll start to think you mean it," he teased.

"What makes you think I don't mean it, you sexy tiger?" Laura flirted back.

"It's been too long, darling." He was getting aroused as he excitedly recalled their occasional past liaisons. "Are we ever going to see each other alone again — just you and I? You know what I mean."

"You naughty boy," giggled Laura. "You know how I like a little variety and spice from time to time. But my number one male doesn't let me out of his sight that often. It sure can be a drag."

"Where's Dave now?"

"He's taking a shower. I'm lying on the bed. We're leaving for a late movie shortly. When we come home, we'll make mad, passionate love," she purred seductively. She heard David switch off the shower. Within seconds he appeared in the bedroom drying his hair. Laura continued, "I really wanted to call and let you know how thrilled we are to be included in your silver wedding anniversary celebration. We'd just love to join you. Be a dear, and please let Sylvia know, won't you? I'm sure we'll see you before your anniversary, but I do hope we will be able to spend some time together while we're in London."

The nuance was not lost on Brian. He knew exactly what she was suggesting. "Goodnight, you little vixen," he cajoled and hung up.

David saw Laura lying on the bed and threw himself on top of her. "Maybe we can skip the movie," he suggested, kissing her softly on the cheeks and caressing her body with his hands.

"Maybe," she mumbled huskily, as she responded positively and encouragingly.

No sooner had Brian placed the phone on the cradle, when it rang again. He picked it up to hear Alicia's voice on the other end of the line. He hadn't spoken to her since her husband's funeral, but knew Sylvia had called frequently since Bruce's death. He immediately felt uneasy.

"Alicia! So good to hear from you. How are you holding up?"

"Well, I have my up days and my down days, thank you. It sure is good to hear your voice, Brian," she said softly.

"Sylvia and I miss you. And, we miss Bruce too," he added slightly clumsily.

"I know," she said quietly. She sensed how awkward Brian was and changed the subject. "I thought it was so very sweet of you both to include me in your anniversary plans."

"Well, I hope you've called to accept. Please say you'll join us. You've been such an important part of our lives for so long. It wouldn't be the same without you."

"Brian, you always did know how to make someone feel special. Actually, I was going to decline, but since you put it like that ..."

Brian interrupted. He heard Sylvia's car pulling into the garage. "Hold on one second. Sylvia's just come home. I'm sure she'd love to have a word with you."

As soon as Sylvia walked through the door, he quickly thrust the telephone receiver into Sylvia's hand, explaining it was Alicia. As the two women continued the conversation, Brian was grateful to be extricated. He decided he wouldn't go out for dinner after all. It was too late and Sylvia was now home. He poured them both a drink. *Maybe, she'll make me a sandwich*, he thought.

Sylvia hung up from Alicia. Brian decided to ignore the disagreement of the night before. He was still reflecting on his exciting phone call with Laura, which had put him in an upbeat frame of mind. It was a giant boost to his ego when women, especially ladies like Laura, still found him attractive. *God, she could be seductive* he thought as he relived some of their few amorous encounters in the past.

"Your hair looks lovely," he said half-heartedly to Sylvia.

"Thank you. Marina and Todd are joining us on the cruise, as is Alicia, which, of course, you probably already know."

"Yes, and Dave and Laura called. They're coming too. I was working a little late tonight when Marshall called from his home. He'd just received your invite and had called the house, but you were out — obviously having your hair done. He will also be coming." He gave his wife a peck on the cheek.

"That just leaves the kids. Did Robin or Stephanie call?"

"Well Stephanie only calls during the day, so she doesn't have to worry about me answering the phone, and you know Robin. He is probably deciding which of his girlfriends is the most suitable to bring before calling."

Sylvia rolled her eyes. Brian decided not to press where Sylvia had been and why she was returning so late. He thought it might be best to let sleeping dogs lie.

"Honey, I haven't eaten. Would you mind making me a sandwich?"

Sylvia thought for a second. The telephone call with Alicia was a reminder of just how tenuous life was and how the widow was having such a tough time without Bruce, trying to carve out a new life for herself. The conversation with Marina that evening during dinner and the changing fortunes of her best friend helped her view things in a new light. She worried about Marina's marriage with Todd and how precarious everything in their lives seemed to be. There was plenty of reason for her to be concerned about both Alicia and Marina. It gave a different perspective of her own life.

"Sure, I'll make you a sandwich," she responded and headed off into the kitchen. "I'll see what I can rustle up."

She was pleased with the enthusiasm Marina had expressed about going on the cruise, and was encouraged by the acceptance of her invite from all their other friends. The memory of the night before when she was toying with cancelling the plans for the trip faded from her mind. The following day was Saturday. She hoped to hear from her children by then. Sylvia would finally be able to start planning the voyage.

CHAPTER 5

The sun from the Sedona sky was streaming down through the bedroom window onto Stephanie's face. She half opened one eye and looked at the clock on the bedside table. It was nine-thirty.

"Jean-Louis! Wake up! We've overslept! It's late!" she exclaimed, shaking her husband.

"It's not late. It's Saturday. Can't we sleep in?" he mumbled, burying his head back in the pillow and hauling the blankets over him.

Stephanie scrambled out of bed and shuffled into the kitchen to make a pot of coffee. As the coffee maker gurgled, she sifted half-heartedly through the unopened mail from the previous day. Jean-Louis emerged from the bedroom yawning and scratching his head and disheveled hair.

"I'd say last night's affair was quite a hit, wouldn't you?"

"Well, your paintings sure were. I was so proud of you." Stephanie put her arms around his neck and they embraced.

"I couldn't have done it without you. All the planning you did — the arranging for the exhibit, sending out the invitations, handling all the food and wine. All I had to do was show up."

"And provide the paintings," Stephanie chuckled. "And, of course, charm the customers, as you always do.

And be the most handsome man in the room." She kissed him again. "It was a huge success. I didn't think the guests would ever leave. I was so exhausted. No wonder we overslept." She poured them both a cup of coffee.

Jean-Louis glanced across the table. "Looks like your mother's handwriting on that envelope."

"So it is." Stephanie picked up the letter and opened it.

"Oh, how exciting, Jean-Louis. It's their silver wedding anniversary, and they want us to join their celebration on the QEII."

"Why is that exciting? Surely you're not going?" He yawned and stretched again.

"Why ever not? Of course we're going."

"Well, your father hasn't spoken to us in over two years for one thing and for another, they didn't attend our wedding."

"Well of course not, we eloped. We need to go for Mother's sake. I love her dearly. As for Dad — well he's just Dad."

"Whatever. We're not going."

Stephanie was taken aback. She knew Jean-Louis was controlling, but was not about to allow him to dictate to her.

"Oh yes, I am going. What's more, you're coming with me," she responded sharply. The immediate hurt look on his face was apparent. "I want you to do this for me, honey." She reached across the table and placed her hands over his. "Please! It's important to me. I want to be there for Mother. She'd be devastated if her only daughter didn't show up."

Jean-Louis pulled his hands away. He stood up,

walked to the window and stared out. He liked things as they were, just the two of them, and a family reunion would be an intrusion. But he knew crossing his wife on this was futile.

"August in Sedona is extremely hot. The business will be closed and it'll be good for us," Stephanie continued. "We've never had a honeymoon. This can be it. It's not like we have to be with the family the whole time."

"And, just when and how do you propose to make up with your father?"

She shrugged. "I won't make a big deal out of it. We probably won't see them before the cruise, so either it will be on board ship or if I speak to him on the phone before then. It'll resolve itself."

"As long as he doesn't start pushing you around, trying to control your life again. If he does, we don't eat with them. We don't speak to them. Nothing. *Rien.* You understand? I can't bear it sometimes the way he talks to you."

Stephanie rose and hugged him. "Everything will be fine. You'll see. Why don't you get showered and dressed while I call Mother?"

"And what if your father answers the phone?"

"Then I'll speak to him. I'm not afraid of him. He has to know Mother would not exclude us from the family affair."

She dialed her mother and, as her childhood and adolescent years in Beverly Hills flashed before her, suddenly felt a little homesick.

"Mother? How are you?"

"Oh, I'm fine, sweetheart. It's lovely to hear from

you. How are you and Jean-Louis?" Sylvia always warmed when she heard from her daughter.

"We're both well, thanks. Sorry I didn't call yesterday. We had an exhibit of Jean-Louis' paintings and I didn't open the mail until this morning."

"Oh, how exciting! How did it go?" Sylvia interjected.

"Mother, it was such a huge success. I so wish you could have been there. But more important, we are both so happy for you and would love to come on the trip. Don't know about spending the few days ahead in London, but we will definitely join you on the cruise."

Sylvia was relieved, since she had wondered whether her daughter's stubborn streak and ongoing estrangement with Brian would deter her. As if reading her mother's thoughts, Stephanie continued. "We wouldn't miss it for the world, Mother. You and Dad making it to twenty-five years," she joked. "And don't worry, I'll resolve things with Dad either beforehand or on the cruise. You'll see."

"I miss you sweetie. Believe it or not, I know your father does too."

Stephanie deflected. "Is Robin coming?"

"We haven't heard from him yet. Sometimes he pops in on Saturday afternoons for tea, before going out and doing whatever it is he does on a Saturday night. He never stays for long. We'll see if he stops by this afternoon. My concern is not whether he will come on the cruise or not, but who he'll bring as his guest if he does."

Sylvia did not have long to wait to find out. As she and Brian were sitting enjoying their tea on the terrace later that day, they saw Robin's sports car speeding up the driveway and grind to a screeching halt. Robin and Jill headed toward the terrace hand in hand.

"Mother, Dad, I'd like you to meet Jill Potts."

Sylvia eyed Jill's appearance with disdain as she shook her hand very briefly. *Such a heavily made-up face and that bleached hair. How cheap*, she thought. The purple and gold toe nails showing through the corked-heeled shoes looked coarse and vulgar. The tight fitting blouse accentuating her ample cleavage and only just covering the top of the shortest of mini-skirts was too much for Sylvia.

"My, my, Robin. Well the apple certainly doesn't fall too far from the tree. You didn't tell me your father was so handsome and such a hunk," Jill offered, shaking Brian's hand while holding it longer than necessary. "Look at that silver hair — so distinguished looking," she gushed. Brian was flattered by this unexpected attention.

"Can I pour you some tea?" Sylvia inquired firmly, offended at the obvious lack of manners.

"I'd prefer a scotch and soda," Jill giggled.

"I'm sure you would. But, right now we are serving tea." Sylvia responded even more tersely.

Robin and Brian exchanged glances. They were only too familiar with the icy tone in Sylvia's voice and knew to tread very softly. This would not be a good meeting.

"Let's all go inside, shall we?" Brian intervened, opening the door for Jill.

Jill ignored the earlier comment from the hostess. "I just *love* how you have decorated your home. Everything's so *perfect*. It's just grand."

"Honey, I'll fetch some extra cups from the kitchen." Brian darted from the room.

There was a brief uncomfortable silence as Jill and Sylvia scrutinized each other.

"Mother, I know it's early, but congratulations to you and Dad on your silver wedding anniversary, and I ... I mean we ... I mean Jill and I would love to accept your offer to join you on the cruise," Robin stammered trying to ease the growing tension.

"I'm so delighted," Sylvia feigned. "I can only imagine how busy it will be for you at the company, so you probably won't be able to spend any time with us in London." It was a statement of fact rather than a question. If it was necessary for her to spend time with Jill, she was determined to keep it to an absolute minimum.

Brian returned with the extra chinaware and Sylvia poured the tea.

"How pretty," Jill observed, picking up her cup.

"So glad you like them. Don't you love Royal Doulton?" Sylvia smiled.

"Royal what?"

Robin jumped in and steered the subject away. "Jill works in a beauty salon."

"I'd never have guessed. Doing what, my dear?" Sylvia interjected, her voice dripping with sarcasm. She was not about to listen to her son's dissertation on Jill's perceived virtues and talents.

"I'm studying for my cosmetology license. I hope to become a manicurist when I'm finished."

"Well, that's a handy profession." Brian laughed

heartily at his own joke. Robin and Jill chuckled along with him. Sylvia remained stone-faced.

Jill reached out for Brian's hands, and began to massage them tenderly. "I could give you a manicure, if you like. No charge. Looks like you sure could use one."

"Thank you, but my husband wouldn't dream of imposing on you, Miss Potts." Sylvia could scarcely believe the temerity. "Pass me your cup. I'm sure you would like some more tea," Sylvia insisted, forcing Jill to release Brian's hand."

"Oh, you must call me Jill. After all, we'll be seeing an awful lot of each other on the cruise."

Sylvia poured more tea, shuddering at the thought.

The stilted conversation continued. After a short while, she took charge.

"I need to see about dinner. You'll both join us, of course?" Sylvia was absolutely certain they wouldn't stay. Knowing Robin's visits on Saturday were never long, maybe she could shorten this one.

"Oh Mother. We can't. We have other plans."

"Oh, I'm so sorry," Sylvia responded insincerely.

"I just wanted you both to meet Jill, and to say how much we are looking forward to the cruise. Come on Jilly, time to go."

Jill picked up the cue and shook hands with Brian and Sylvia. "So nice to have met you both — finally. I was beginning to wonder if you actually existed or whether you were part of Robin's imagination," she giggled.

Sylvia and Brian stood in the doorway as Robin and Jill made their way down the terrace steps and climbed into the car. Sylvia turned to go into the house.

"Your father is a very sexy man, and so *cute*," Jill purred to Robin as he started the engine. She smiled and winked at Brian, blew him a kiss and waved to him as the car revved and screeched toward the gate.

Brian followed his wife into the house. "Can I pour you a drink, dear?"

"I certainly need one after that."

"Did you have to be so cold to her?"

"She made such a blatant pass at you, how was I expected to react? I have no idea where Robin finds these cheap looking tramps. I surely don't know what he sees in them."

I do. Oh indeed, I do, Brian thought, still feeling the softness of Jill's hand. He kept his musings and imaginings to himself as he poured his wife a glass of sherry.

CHAPTER 6

Sylvia was thrilled to receive acceptances to all her invitations and immediately contacted her travel agent to handle the QEII reservations. She wanted to ensure that she and Brian, as well as her guests, had the best cabins available, so time was of the essence. Much to her delight, she was able to obtain exactly the desired suites, and set about arranging the accommodation.

Brian seemed more interested in this trip than most of the others she had planned, but was dismissive when Sylvia explained the complexities.

"Well, it's not easy to arrange the dinner seating plans and all the cabin assignments. It's more complicated than you think," she said.

"What are our cabins like?" he asked curiously.

"Well, the nice thing is, we are on the Signal Deck. There are two Grand Suites. I've reserved one for us — the Queen Elizabeth Suite. I reserved six Queen Anne's and one Queen Victoria. Each of them has a balcony. I've no idea who will occupy the other Grand Suite."

"Why did you reserve only one Queen Victoria and six Queen Anne suites? What's the difference?"

"None whatsoever. The Queen Anne's are one side of the corridor and the Victoria suites are on the other. The first Queen Anne Suite is next to ours. I've reserved that for Stephanie and Jean-Louis. Across the corridor is the Queen Victoria, which is identical to the Queen Anne.

I've reserved that for Robin. That way, our children can be close by."

Brian thought for a moment. "Why are we paying for eight suites when there are only twelve of us going?"

"Well, surely you don't expect Marshall and Alicia to share a suite? I have placed Marshall in the suite next to Stephanie and Jean-Louis, Marina and Todd next to him followed by Laura and David. Alicia will be at the end, and on the other side of staircase will be Miss Potts."

"Surely we're not paying for a separate suite for Jill? Besides, you can't put her at the other side of the staircase all by herself."

"I have no intention of promoting the relationship between Robin and Miss Potts. To put her in the same suite as Robin would be tantamount to sanctioning their tawdry relationship, which is simply out of the question. Besides, it would be most presumptuous of us to assume she would find sharing a cabin with Robin acceptable."

"Well, at least put Robin and Jill closer together. Why can't she have the vacant suite next to Robin's?"

"Absolutely not," Sylvia replied firmly. "I'm sure Robin's friend will find her accommodations most suitable and amenable."

"Look, darling," Brian pleaded. "Please try and make a little effort to be pleasant to Jill. She is Robin's choice, after all. If she makes him happy, isn't that what matters?"

"I wish you'd apply the same sense of logic to Stephanie and Jean-Louis. Look how long it is since you have spoken to them. You've made Jean-Louis most unwelcome in the family and ostracized Stephanie at the same time."

Brian shrugged. He hated it when Sylvia got the better

of him in a discussion. He knew she was right and deftly changed the subject.

"How is the dinner seating plan coming along? Please tell me you haven't put me next to that dreadful Todd?"

"Of course not." She was relieved they would not get into yet another confrontation over their son's girlfriend. "You will be seated at one end and I at the head on the other end. You will have Robin and Miss Potts either side of you."

Brian raised his eyes.

"Stephanie and Jean-Louis will be seated either side of me." Noting the perplexed look on Brian's face, she continued.

"It's appropriate we have our children next to us, and you know I always prefer spouses and partners to sit opposite each other. Given that you still haven't cleared the air with Stephanie, and since you seemingly approve of Miss Potts, it seemed natural for her and Robin to be at your end, and Stephanie and Jean-Louis by me. Todd has been placed next to Stephanie, and Marina next to Jean-Louis. That will relieve you of having to make conversation with Todd. Alicia and Marshall are seated in the middle with David and Laura sitting next to Robin and Miss Potts."

"At least you could stop calling her Miss Potts, couldn't you? Her name is Jill. You can't possibly go through an entire two weeks calling her Miss Potts."

"I'm still hoping that by some happy chance, Robin will have a change of heart and find a new girlfriend. Apart from the obvious unsuitability, there's just something about her that doesn't sit right. Look how she behaved when she was over here the first time. And let's not forget the last time she came here, she practically threw herself at you. She was like a bitch in heat."

"Well, why should that surprise you? At least, with your mutual attraction to me, you have something in common," Brian responded, trying to make light of the subject.

Sylvia was not amused and ignored his remarks.

"We will be dining in the Mauritania Restaurant. I was hoping for the Queen's Grill, which is where they normally seat people from the Signal Deck, but the staff can't seat all of us at one table. I don't care for the idea of having us seated separately."

"Knowing you, I'm sure everything will be perfect." Brian hugged her.

Sylvia continued to work feverishly on the planning and preparations for her grand adventure. She knew the next couple of months would be exhausting with no end to the details requiring her attention.

"Darling, there's only a dozen of us going. It's not the entire 'Royal Household' and their entourage that's travelling," Brian would say as he observed Sylvia totally absorbed in every facet of the trip.

"If it were, it would be the responsibility of an entire staff. Since it is not, it is I who has to handle all the planning," she always retorted as she busied herself with the phone calls, the letters, and the shopping. But she enjoyed it.

Brian knew the occasion was in capable hands, and occupied himself with business affairs he would attend to while in London. He held never-ending telephone discussions with the managers from the various offices throughout England and Scotland, insisting they all travel to London for an all-day meeting coinciding with his visit.

He knew, too, while Sylvia never cared for any of Robin's girlfriends, she particularly disliked Jill. This disturbed him, as Sylvia's instincts and intuitions were generally solid. He called his private investigator.

"Jack, I'd like you to do a little background check on a young lady named Jill Potts. No, nothing serious. She works as a manicurist in Beverly Hills. No, she lives here, but is not from California originally. Can you check and see what you can find out about her? You know, family, childhood, any criminal record, past relationships etcetera. See what you can get for me in the next month or so, will you? Thanks, Jack."

It would help if he knew a little more about her background. He hoped to have the information before they left on the trip, just in case there was anything troublesome. Nonetheless, he could see why his son liked her. He was also astute enough to know when someone was trying to seduce him. There was no doubt Jill was flirting with him. Sylvia was right about that.

As he rocked back and forth in his office chair fantasizing over a lascivious little fling with Jill, the private phone rang in his office. Laura was at the other end of the line.

"Well, are we going to have any time together in London? As the song says, *big spender, I can show you a good time*," Laura teased demurely.

"Now, how can I pass up an invitation like that?" Brian snapped back to reality.

"You can't."

"Well, the second day in London I have an all-day business meeting, but maybe the first day, I could arrange for David to be at the recording studio. Perhaps you and I can get together for a little coffee or something."

"I think I'd prefer the 'or something'," she giggled.

"It's a deal," he chuckled. "Lunch with Laura."

"Dessert with Brian."

Brian laughed again. "I'll make a note."

"Now why don't you just do that?" Laura responded seductively, and hung up the phone.

I've a feeling this trip will be quite an exciting adventure in more ways than one, Brian thought. He dialed his office in London to book the recording studio for David the day after their arrival.

CHAPTER 7

Finally, the day of the departure arrived. Brian played a round of golf, while Sylvia visited the salon to have her hair tinted.

She had made certain that everything was packed the night before, so nothing would be rushed. Both she and Brian enjoyed the light snack Helen had prepared for them, after which Sylvia readied herself in eager anticipation of the adventure that lay ahead. However, her natural English reserve prevented her from being overly expressive as she maintained her composure sitting at the vanity table dabbing her cheeks with pale rouge.

Brian could barely contain his boyish exuberance, as he darted about excitedly. "Darling, did you remember to pack my special cologne? Do you have my blood pressure pills?"

"Yes dear. Stop worrying."

"Did you speak to Robin about driving us to the airport? Do you have my passport in your handbag?"

"*Yes,*" she responded. "Everything is taken care of. Trust me."

Brian stopped for a moment, watched her applying her make-up in the mirror and marveled at her. There was no doubt in his mind she had paid meticulous attention to all the details. He knew there would be no hitches on the trip. Sylvia was the consummate organizer. He had always been grateful and admired her for that.

Brian's sole contribution to the trip would be to find the appropriate silver wedding gift for her. He knew he would need to look no further than Aspreys in London. With its reputation for supplying the finest jewelry to the world's royalty, he would find her the perfect gift and was pleased Sylvia had suggested spending time in London.

He moved toward where Sylvia was sitting and leaned over, hugging her from behind. "I do love you," he whispered to her tenderly.

She looked at his reflection in the mirror and patted his hand. "I know. Now hurry up and get ready. Robin will be here soon."

She rose, and left him behind as she headed toward the drawing room, where she ticked off all the items on her prepared check list: passports, plane tickets, hotel confirmations and other such details. While waiting for Robin to arrive, she called Alicia and Stephanie to wish them safe journeys and tell them she was looking forward to seeing them on board ship in a few days' time.

The sudden screeching of brakes in the driveway alerted her to Robin's arrival. *His fast driving will be the death of him — and me,* she thought, picking up her handbag and making her way to the front door and onto the porch.

"You're looking great, Mother," Robin effused, bounding up the steps and kissing her on the cheek. "Where's Dad?"

"I'm here, Son." Brian emerged from the house carrying the suitcases.

As the two men loaded the luggage into the trunk,

Sylvia positioned herself in the back seat. She opened her compact, looked in the mirror and adjusted her hair slightly.

"Please try and drive a little slower, Robin. We have plenty of time," she admonished as he sped off.

Surprisingly, they all noted, there were no traffic jams or accidents as they headed toward the airport and arrived there with ample time to spare.

Robin hugged his father. "Goodbye, Dad." He turned to his mother and smiled. "Safe trip, Mother. See you in a few days." They kissed each other on the cheek. "Oh, and Mother, please try and be nice to Jilly. She is looking forward to this trip so much," he pleaded gently.

"And when have I not been nice to any of your girlfriends?" she shot back.

Robin smiled weakly, decided discretion was the better part of valor, and allowed the question to go unanswered.

"Come along, darling." Brian took Sylvia by the arm, and they headed to the first class check-in desk. Within minutes they were in the British Airways lounge and were surprised to see Marina and Todd, Laura and David already waiting.

There were greetings and hugs all around as an atmosphere of festivity and jubilation suddenly pervaded the air around them.

"Oh Sylvia, you look wonderful," gushed Marina.

"Simply fabulous," Laura agreed, while sneaking a sly wink at Brian. Brian responded in kind, knowing no one noticed. "Thank you so much for including us in such a special celebration," Laura continued. "We can't tell you how much we're looking forward to it, can we, Dave?"

David nodded in agreement. "It's going to be splendid. Just splendid."

"Well, let's celebrate then," Brian said heartily. "Where's the bubbly?"

Todd, always ready for a drink, walked to the bar and poured six glasses of champagne. David helped him carry them back to the table.

Brian raised his glass in a toast, and turned to Sylvia. "Here's to my wife of almost twenty five years. I salute you." The group chimed in. "To Sylvia!"

Sylvia grinned, slightly embarrassed, but glowed in the spotlight, nonetheless. The chatter and conversation flowed like the champagne, helping them to pass the time while they waited to board their flight to London.

Once they were in their first class seats, Sylvia laid her head back on the headrest as Brian reached out and held her hand. She closed her eyes as she anticipated her months of planning coming to fruition.

It was a slightly overcast day as the plane touched down at Heathrow Airport the next morning and the sun struggled to peek through the clouds. Pleasantly surprised at the alacrity with which they all were able to proceed through customs and immigration, Sylvia was relieved to see the limousine service she had arranged awaiting their arrival.

"I'd forgotten how green everything is in England," observed Marina, looking at the fields and meadows as they were transported along the motorway to their hotel in the heart of the city.

"Yes, quite delightful, isn't it?" Sylvia agreed.

The limousine quietly and slowly made its way through the noisy bustle of the London traffic, past Harrods, around Green Park and along Park Lane, finally pulling into the entrance of the famed Dorchester Hotel.

The stone-faced doorman, replete in his long coat, doffed his top hat as he opened the door of the limousine. Brian stepped out first and helped the ladies from the vehicle. David and Todd followed and led the way into the hotel while Brian took care of the limousine driver.

Sylvia was pleased their roof suites were adjacent, and all had the terrace balconies she'd requested. Their panoramic views overlooking the parks, London, and its skyline were simply spectacular. She stood for a moment thinking of the land of her childhood, and the journey her life had taken. Brian joined her on the terrace and they shared a moment as they observed the people, looking like thousands of ants, walking in the park across the street. They watched and listened to the mighty roar of the traffic whizzing up and down Park Lane.

⁕

In the suite next door, Todd headed to the minibar, poured himself a drink, and settled on the sofa.

"It's only just noon." chided Marina gently. "Do you have to drink so soon — and so early?"

"All I heard from Dave on the flight are all the interviews he has lined up while he is in London. He's on this TV show, that radio show, a guest appearance for some charity function, a session at the recording studio. I'm sick of it."

Marina sat next to him, running her fingers slowly through his hair. She pitied her husband and worried about his frame of mind. But their financial burdens were never far from her thoughts, as she tried in her own way to keep their expenses to a minimum. "I'm sure things will change once your contract is renewed."

"That's another thing. Why hasn't Brian said anything about the contract yet?"

Marina shrugged. "Maybe you can find a moment while we're on the cruise and discuss it with him. I'm sure it's just an oversight. Anyway, I thought Marshall handled all the contracts?"

"Marshall writes all the contracts and signs them, but Brian always looks over them for review. Supposedly, it is just a formality. Marshall told me it's on Brian's desk, and has been for at least a month."

"Well, Brian has been busy. You know that. Everything will be fine, you'll see." She tried to sound convincing, but even she was beginning to have her doubts.

David was busy unpacking and putting his clothes in the drawers, while Laura removed her shoes and slipped out of her travelling attire.

"Honey, are you going shopping tomorrow while I'm at the studio?"

Laura shrugged. "I don't know. I guess I hadn't thought too much about it. "

"I just assumed you were going to Harrods with Sylvia."

"I thought maybe I would come with you to the studio," she lied. She knew full well what she would be doing the next day.

"Why, honey, I think that would be just wonderful." He stopped his unpacking, and kissed her on the forehead.

His response startled her. She had never attended one of his recording sessions and he had never asked her to be there. *Damn*, she thought. *Now I'll have to fake a migraine headache.*

She smiled, and quickly changed the subject. "Let's take a nap, before I shower and freshen up. Sylvia wants us to meet her at three-thirty for afternoon tea."

"Good idea. I hardly slept on the plane."

As it was, everyone overslept and missed the renowned tea. After a flurry of phone calls, Sylvia arranged for all to meet for cocktails in the bar at 6:30 followed by dinner at 7:30.

Knowing it was 5:00 p.m. in London, she realized it was 9:00 a.m. where Robin and Stephanie were, a good time to call her children to let them know they had arrived safely.

She was somewhat surprised to hear Jill answer the phone at Robin's house.

"I just can't wait to see you next week — and Brian," Jill giggled. "We're going to have so much fun. Robin and I are simply thrilled to be joining you on this cruise. It's like, Wow!"

"Well, my husband and I hope the cruise meets your expectations," Sylvia responded crisply. "We'd certainly hate for *you* to be disappointed. Is my son there?"

"Sure thing. Bye-bye now." She turned to Robin. "Honey, it's your mom."

Robin took the phone from Jill. "Hi, Mother. You arrived safely? Have a good flight?"

"Thank you, dear. It was fine. Just wanted to let you know we all arrived safely without problems. We're getting ready for dinner now."

"Thanks for the call, Mother. See you next week."

Sylvia hung up and dialed Stephanie, and was pleased to hear her daughter's voice. *What a refreshing change to have the phone answered by someone with couth*, she thought.

"Just wanted you to know we arrived safely. The hotel suites are gorgeous. I can't wait to see you next week, sweetie."

"I can't either, Mother. We have a surprise for you. I have some wonderful news, but I can't tell you now. Must go. Thanks for the call. Love you." She hung up.

"I love you too, baby," Sylvia responded to the sound of the dial tone, as she placed the receiver back in the cradle. She speculated about the news Stephanie had. She wondered whether she and Brian were to become grandparents — and pondered how Brian would deal with the first grandchild not coming from his son, as well as his intense dislike for Jean-Louis. Then again, maybe the news was that they would be moving back to California, or maybe Jean-Louis' paintings were doing well and they were moving to a larger studio.

She heard Brian whistling away in the shower. *Probably best to keep the conversation with Stephanie to myself for the time being* she thought as she finished readying herself for dinner.

CHAPTER 8

For dinner their first night in London, Sylvia had picked *The Nightingale* in the heart of Mayfair, around the corner from Berkley Square.

"So who is going to join me tomorrow for a shopping spree at Harrods?" she asked gaily, enjoying the splendor of the evening.

"Oh, I'm afraid we can't. Todd and I are taking the train to Windsor to visit my cousin for the day," Marina replied. Todd rolled his eyes, and took another gulp of his whiskey.

"I won't be able to join you either. I'm going to the recording studio with David. I'm so excited. I can hardly wait. In all the years we've been married, I've never been inside a recording studio. Imagine that!" Laura looked at her husband adoringly, and put her arm through his.

"Oh dear! Looks like I will be shopping alone." Sylvia appeared crestfallen. She turned to Brian. "I suppose you have meetings while you're here, dear?"

"Ah, yes. And you know me and shopping. Besides, you never like me shopping with you."

Sylvia had to admit that was true. During her shopping excursion to Harrods, she didn't want her husband looking at his watch every two minutes, asking how much longer she would be.

"Perhaps we could all meet for afternoon tea at Fortnum's at four o'clock?"

"If we're back in time, we'd love to join you," Marina enthused.

"If we're finished with the recording session, count on us," David chimed in.

"Of course we'll be finished recording. I'm sure you'll do everything in one take," Laura added.

"I'll be there if I can," echoed Brian.

Sylvia was pleased with how the trip was progressing so far. All was going according to plan.

"Darling, I have such a splitting headache this morning, would you mind awfully if I didn't go with you today?" Laura yelled to David.

"Oh no. It's not one of your migraines, is it?" David emerged from the bathroom, towel around his waist, still with the razor in his hand and shaving cream on his face. He went to stroke his wife's head.

"It certainly feels like one. I hope it'll wear off. I was *so* looking forward to going to the studio with you." Laura feigned a pout.

"Maybe I should stay here with you."

She sat up in bed. "Of course not. I want you to record your next hit song. You must go to the studio. Besides, all those musicians are there. It would be terrible if you didn't go. You can't just not show up."

David finished getting ready, kissed his wife on the forehead, and reluctantly left for the studio alone. As he got off the elevator, he bumped into Sylvia, who had been enjoying breakfast with Brian at the Promenade.

"Where's Laura?" Sylvia inquired.

"Oh, she has one of her wretched migraine headaches again."

"What a shame. She seemed to be looking forward to going with you today."

The doorman hailed a cab.

They were heading in separate directions across the city, so David helped Sylvia into her taxicab, before getting into his own.

Sylvia loved the all too familiar black taxi cabs that were so much part of London and its history, and soon struck up a light, informal conversation with the Cockney cabbie.

It was not far from the Dorchester to Harrods and Sylvia was soon wandering around her most favorite department store in the whole world.

Brian, safe in the knowledge his wife would be at Harrods for the better part of the day, and having seen David jump in the next taxicab from his vantage point in the Promenade, sipped his coffee for a safe amount of time, finished reading the newspaper, and headed upstairs to his suite. He called Maureen and Todd on the telephone to make sure there had not been a change in their plans. He was relieved when there was no reply. It meant they were on their way to Windsor. He called Laura.

"The coast is clear and the door is unlocked," Laura purred demurely.

"You little vixen," Brian chided, and headed for the room next door, flipping the "Do Not Disturb" sign as he entered.

"I could have at least accompanied David and Laura to the studio," Todd complained as the train chugged its way out of London, through the suburbs and into the countryside. "Maybe, I would have made some contacts, met some old business acquaintances, and at least gotten my foot in the door."

"It would have been obvious what you were trying to do. The dislike you and David have for each other is almost palpable. In any event, your just showing up would have alienated Brian. If he'd have wanted you there, he would have asked. Better find a time on the ship alone when you can discuss your contract. Right now, let's just enjoy a day with my cousin."

"I don't know if Brian will even be at the studio today. I thought he was going to his office."

"We're on vacation. It's time you stopped worrying and started to relax."

Todd flopped back on the seat and watched the scenery go by, not relishing the day with Maureen's prim and proper relatives. He hoped Sylvia's invitation to afternoon tea at Fortnum's would have them heading back to London early.

It was almost lunchtime, and Sylvia pondered having lunch. She had suddenly become very drowsy, and wondered whether it was jetlag, change of air, or just her body relaxing after having been through such a frantic pace the last couple of months. Whatever the reason, she decided to return to the hotel and enjoy a nap before going to afternoon tea. Besides, shopping wasn't quite as much fun without Marina or Laura. On her way out she stopped by the pharmacy to see if she could find any pills that might help Laura. Of course, Laura probably travelled with some, but just in case she didn't.

"What do you recommend for acute migraine headaches?"

The pharmacist steered her to some over the counter tablets, and Sylvia selected a jar. She noticed an ornate, attractive little pill box. *How cute*, she thought. "I'll take one of these adorable little boxes too, please," she advised the attendant. She paid the bill and headed for the Harrods exit.

Arriving back at The Dorchester, she headed past her suite to the one occupied by David and Laura. As she raised her hand to knock on the door, she noticed the "Do Not Disturb" sign and stood back for a second, wondering whether to proceed to get the pills to Laura, or wait until later.

She was taken aback when she heard what sounded like Brian's voice emanating from the suite.

"Laura, I *must* go. I have to go and buy Sylvia's anniversary gift."

"Oh Brian, can't you buy it tomorrow? Who knows when we will have another opportunity like this?"

"I have an all day meeting tomorrow. Besides, David will be around, and who knows what Sylvia will be doing?"

"So there's nothing more I can do to tempt you to stay?" Laura was being at her seductive best.

"You've already done more than enough."

"Oh, c'mon. Why go and buy jewels? I have perfect treasure for you here," she taunted.

"You're insatiable."

Hearing the sound of footsteps approaching the door, Sylvia ran to the end of the corridor, and turned the corner, still within an earshot.

She heard the door to the suite open, and recognized Laura's voice.

"Goodbye my passionate one."

"Goodbye my little vixen."

She heard the sound of their kissing, the sound of Brian's heavy footsteps heading toward the elevator, and then the sound of the elevator doors opening.

"David! What are you doing back so soon?" Brian was startled.

"I have to return to the studios tomorrow. They're re-working a couple of the musical arrangements. I've got a few recordings in the can though. I thought you were going to your office today?"

"Yes. I was," Brian stammered. "But I left early. I'm heading to Aspreys to get Sylvia's anniversary gift. See you later." He pressed the elevator button and the doors closed. *What a close shave* Brian thought, heaving a huge sigh of relief.

David headed toward the suite, and was surprised to see the "Do Not disturb" sign on the door. *Maybe Laura had asked the cleaners to put it on the door for her.* He unlocked the door and entered the room quietly, in case she was sleeping. As he moved toward the verandah, he was shocked to see a view of her back. She was wearing a diaphanous negligee and not the plain cotton nightgown she was wearing when he left that morning.

"Well, I see your headache has disappeared," he said, somewhat mystified.

Startled, Laura swung around, revealing a champagne glass in her hand. "David! What are you doing back so early?"

"Never mind that. What on earth are you doing drinking champagne? " he demanded angrily.

Laura fluffed her hair, totally caught off guard. "I was waiting for you to come home, my darling," she stumbled unconvincingly.

"Nonsense! You know full well we were meeting Sylvia for tea at four o'clock and I would have gone straight there. It was only because of recording problems at the studio that I came back here to see how you were."

He noticed the guilty look on Laura's face. "What the hell is going on?"

Laura put her glass down, and quickly moved toward him, throwing her arms around his neck. As she went to kiss him, he pushed her away. For the first time, he saw a second champagne glass on the table. It suddenly occurred to him Brian had not inquired about Laura's whereabouts when they met at the elevator, and Brian had known Laura was accompanying him to the studio.

"That's Brian's glass, isn't it? Brian was here."

Laura stood in front of him and nodded slowly. "But, it's not what you think." She moved toward him again. "I love you, David. You know that."

"Oh my God. I don't believe it." David was dumbfounded. He ran his fingers through his hair as he paced back and forth across the room.

Laura tried to get to him to calm him down.

"Jesus Christ. I don't bloody believe it! You're cheating on me with Brian, my best friend." He banged his clenched fists against the wall.

Laura had never seen David like this, and was uncertain how to handle him.

"You're not going to tell Sylvia?" she asked quietly.

David exploded. "Sylvia? Sylvia? You're now showing concern for Sylvia? Why the hell didn't you think about Sylvia earlier? It's her silver wedding anniversary, you are her guest and one of her best friends, and you are doing who-knows-what with her husband. I can't believe you would do such a thing. You don't even seem concerned about us." David was furious. Silence fell as David roamed the room like a caged tiger.

"What are you going to do?" Laura asked meekly. David stared at his wife.

"I don't know. Right now, I am going out to get some air and think. One thing is for sure. I wouldn't dream of hurting Sylvia's feelings. She is too much of a classy lady and good friend to have her dream trip ruined. We'll have to go ahead with the cruise. I don't know how you and Brian can live with yourselves. I could kill you both. How the hell can you even face Sylvia?" He stormed out of the room, slamming the door behind him.

Sylvia had heard David enter his room, and had quickly run to her suite. She opened the door to the verandah to let some air in, and had heard the entire conversation between Laura and David.

She was shattered. Despite the rumors that had persisted about Brian's infidelities over the years, it had never been so patently clear to her as it was that moment. *God, I sacrificed my career and everything for this man*, she thought as her mind rolled back through the years. She had always been able to push unpleasant thoughts and suspicions out of her mind, but this one was like a slap in the face. Brian definitely was having an affair — and with one of her dearest friends.

How long had it been going on? What was she to do? Should she cancel the trip? Should she confront Brian and Laura? Sylvia sat on the side of the bed, and sobbed uncontrollably at the cruel turn of events. She suddenly felt very alone.

CHAPTER 9

Denise Parker looked out her window as her plane touched down at Gatwick Airport and hoped her good friend, Irma, was there to meet her as promised. She had decided not to arrive at the Southampton docks in a stretch limousine which would have drawn attention to her arrival. Far better her friend drive her there in more modest transport, in order to be inconspicuous when boarding the ship. Donning her large dark sunglasses and long fur coat with its matching hat, she thought *It may be summer in England, but it's always as cold as the Arctic.* She knew to dress right.

"Darling, how wonderful to see you," Irma said in a low tone upon greeting Denise after she cleared customs. They kissed each other on both cheeks, and Irma helped Denise with the luggage to the car. They were soon speeding along the motorway in Irma's understated Audi. *Perfect*, Denise thought. It was not a car to attract too much notice.

Irma was a true slice of old England, and was British to the core. She had a gentle face, pale blue eyes, and pinkish cheeks to accentuate her typically English complexion. She was a real country lass who, along with her husband, enjoyed her rural lifestyle with their dogs and horses.

"I don't know what you are up to, Denise. I'm not sure if I even want to know. But I must say, it is all rather mysterious. You arriving here like this. So incognito. It's not like you to arrive without fanfare. And why couldn't you have spent a few days with Johnnie and me in the country?" she pleaded. "We'd love to have you."

Denise smiled. "You're right, Irma. You don't want to know what I'm up to. I wouldn't bore you with it anyway. But I do promise to come back and spend some more time with you."

"I'm going to hold you to that promise, and make sure you keep it," Irma said firmly.

"How is Johnnie?" Denise changed the subject.

The two chatted incessantly about their lives for the duration of the ride and arrived at the docks in plenty of time for Denise be one of the first to board ship and avoid arriving at the same time as Brian and Sylvia. As she walked up the gangway there were no other passengers in sight. She quickly found the Grand Suite she had reserved and locked herself inside. She was impressed with the elegance of the suite, and loved the beautifully large floral arrangement, compliments of the management of the cruise line. She knew instinctively her suite was across from Brian and Sylvia's, and wondered how many rooms along the corridor they had booked for their entourage.

There was a knock at the door and the porter entered the suite with her luggage. She tipped him, removed her boots, closed the drapes, and lay down for a short nap. As usual, she had not slept well on the flight, and appreciated the spacious suite and calm now surrounding her. She had plenty of time to prepare for her surprise and unannounced performance that evening, knowing what songs in her repertoire she would be singing.

She awoke with a jolt a few hours later to the sound of the brass band playing on the quayside. There was much noise in the corridor of people going back and forth; and she tried to decipher the voices amongst the chatter. Below, the drums pounded and the bugles blared their patriotic British songs. She wanted to venture out onto the deck and throw the paper streamers and join in the departure festivities, but knew it could jeopardize her planned surprise. The cacophony along the corridor subsided, and she listened to the stirring songs from below, as she tapped her fingers on the blanket in time to the music. *The beat and rhythm needs to be a little faster* she thought.

Sylvia had arranged for two limousines to transport everyone from London to Southampton. Marshall and Alicia had arrived the night before and shared the limousine with David and Laura, Marina and Todd to Southampton. The day the cruise departed, Stephanie and Jean-Louis' flight arrived at London Heathrow Airport within an hour of Robin and Jill's flight. Sylvia insisted that she and Brian be at the airport with the limousine to meet them.

With her amazing ability to delay unpleasant decisions, Sylvia decided to postpone the handling of her situation with Brian until they returned to Beverly Hills, as the cruise would give her time to think of a long term plan. In the meantime, she would retain her dignity, and treat Laura as if nothing had happened. She had enough to contend with ensuring Stephanie and her father made their peace.

Brian sensed something was not quite right with his wife. He had not been married to her for twenty-five years without knowing something about her moods and emotions, but he did not press her. He disliked confrontations as much as she did, and assumed it was Sylvia having to deal with Jill and the anxiety that everything would go according to plan on the trip. He also knew Sylvia was annoyed that he and Stephanie had not spoken before leaving America. In deference to Sylvia, he decided to make the first move with his estranged daughter hoping that would please his wife.

He stretched out his arms and hugged his daughter. "It's wonderful to see you, princess! Thanks for sharing our special anniversary with us." Stephanie knew her Dad's gestures were perfunctory and responded in kind. Knowing he was being cordial for her mother's sake, she adopted the same posture.

Brian shook hands with Jean-Louis. "Good to see you. How are things in the art world?"

Sylvia embraced them both. "It's good seeing the two of you. It's been too long. You don't know how much it means to me to have you both here."

"And how much it means to me, too," added Brian. Sylvia shot him a glance.

"How was your flight?" Sylvia continued.

"It was fine. We were almost an hour late taking off, but knew Robin was arriving an hour later, so we weren't too concerned. As we were waiting for our luggage, we saw Robin standing in line with his passport the other side of the immigration counter. I assume that was Jill who was draped all over him." Stephanie responded.

Jean-Louis interjected. "It was so nice of you both to include me for such an auspicious occasion."

"We wouldn't have thought of excluding you, would we darling?" Sylvia turned to Brian.

Brian looked past his wife. "Here come Robin and Jill now." He waved towards his son, and left the group to meet them.

Sylvia eyed Brian as he hugged his son and embraced Jill for a little longer than she thought appropriate.

Robin kissed his mother. "Hi Sis," he said to Stephanie giving her a small hug. He nodded to Jean-Louis.

"I'd like you both to meet Jill."

Stephanie's eyes dressed Jill up and down, as Jill stepped closer to hug her.

"Can I give your husband a hug, Steffie?" Jill chuckled, and not waiting for a response, "I think I'll give him a hug anyway. French men are just so sexy, aren't they?"

"The name is Stephanie," was the terse reply, as she developed an instant dislike to her brother's girlfriend. *What trash, and so typical of Robin*, she thought.

"The limousine's waiting," Sylvia intervened. "Shall we go? Remember, we all have a ship to catch." She smiled uneasily.

The conversation was stilted during the drive.

"I'm sure we're just going to be the best of friends, Stephanie," Jill enthused, while filing her nails.

"I'll look forward to that. I'm sure we have so much in common," Stephanie answered drily.

Brian picked up on his daughter's sarcasm, a trait he

knew she inherited from her mother. He changed the subject.

"Jean-Louis, you never did tell me how the art business is doing."

"Yeah, has the Pope called you yet to re-paint the Sistine Chapel?" Robin chided. He cared less for his brother-in-law than he did his sister.

"No, he hasn't. But then he's probably too busy spending an inordinate amount of time saying prayers for forgiveness of your many sins," shot back Stephanie.

"Ha! Ha! Very funny, Sis."

"Can you two just simmer down and knock it off?" Brian asked.

"Your father's right," said Jill. "Have you forgotten? This is a special occasion. It's your parent's anniversary. We're all supposed to be happy, right?" She looked around at everyone.

"Why, thank you Miss Potts. Nice of you to remind us all," Sylvia noted.

"Oh please, call me Jill. I've told you that before."

"You're absolutely right. I'm so sorry — Jill." Sylvia bowed her head slightly.

Brian rubbed his hands together. "Well, it's not long now until we will be partying up a storm on board ship."

"I'm sure we will all have a wonderful time," Jean-Louis acknowledged uncomfortably.

The limousine purred along the motorway to its destination.

By the time the ship was ready to set sail the luggage had not arrived in all the cabins, but the Sinclairs, along with their friends and family, were all out on deck throwing the streamers overboard and tapping their feet to the songs being played by the band. Brian engaged himself in a dance twirl with Sylvia, who protested the shoes she was wearing weren't right for dancing. Todd was singing along quietly to Marina with his arm around her shoulder. Jean-Louis kissed his wife lovingly on her forehead. David was subdued as he looked at the band below, Laura tucking her arm in his, not knowing what to do to make things right. She did love her husband. She had just wanted an element of excitement in her life.

"Isn't this just so much fun?" squealed Jill excitedly as she was throwing the streamers. Her ample cleavage showed as Robin salivated from behind.

Marshall was standing next to Alicia. "Come on, Alicia. You can throw better than that."

"I'm trying my best, Marshall," Alicia laughed. She was pleased she came along and was thankful Sylvia and Brian had thought to include her. It was exactly the tonic she needed, precisely what Sylvia told her it would be.

The sun was slowly setting behind them, and there was a slight crispness in the air. Sylvia was glad when she heard the foghorns and noticed the ship pull away slowly from the dockside. They all watched together as the band players became smaller and smaller in the distance until they looked like ants.

"Come on everyone. Let's go inside and dress for dinner. It's chilly out here. You must be freezing in that top, Jill," Sylvia admonished.

"I doubt that," Stephanie muttered looking at the low cut neckline of Jill's blouse. "She's like a cat on a hot tin roof."

"Dinner at eight in the Mauritania, everyone. See you for cocktails at seven," announced Sylvia, taking charge.

There was a chorus of "See you later," and "Looking forward to it," as they all departed inside their respective cabins to freshen up and change for dinner.

Robin was miffed his cabin was so far down the other end of the corridor from Jill's. *So typical of Mother*, he thought, shaking his head.

CHAPTER 10

Brian was rummaging around in his suitcase. "Honey, I can't find my cologne. Where did you pack it?"

"It's already unpacked and in the bathroom cabinet." Sylvia wondered how he would cope with many of the merest basics in life if she weren't around.

Brian strode to the bathroom, and Sylvia heard him splashing the cologne on his face. He whistled while he checked whether his hair needed more combing and, observing a few grey strands, contemplated whether he should start coloring it. He returned to the living area as Sylvia emerged fully dressed wearing a soft, understated, lavender, satin evening gown, amethyst earrings and necklace, carrying an ermine stole.

Brian gasped. "Darling, you look simply stunning. Simply stunning. You will be the belle of the ball this evening. But then you always are." He kissed her on the cheeks.

Sylvia looked at her husband in his tuxedo. He was just as handsome and still possessed the same boyish charm she fell in love with all those years ago. She was confused as she juggled in her mind his act of betrayal, and the man in front of her with whom she was so deeply in love.

"Thank you. Shall we go?" Sylvia smiled placing her hand through his arm, and they headed toward the Mauritania bar.

They were first to arrive. Sylvia went to check the restaurant and confirm the seating positions had been assigned according to her instructions. The floral centerpiece the QEII had provided was as elegant as she had been assured it would be. The arrangement, a mass of white roses, virtually covered the entire length of the table. Much of the greenery, as well as the flowers, were sprinkled with silver and a few silver ornaments adorned the arrangement. She smiled at the miniature silver hearts, bells, wedding chapel, champagne glasses, and wedding cake complete with bride and groom, all strategically placed and dramatizing the setting. The table layout exceeded even her expectations and Sylvia was pleased.

She returned to the bar and observed the rest of the group coming along the corridor toward her. Everyone, except for Robin and Jill.

"Sylvia. You look magnificent. Where did you get that gorgeous dress?" Alicia exclaimed.

"Yes, do tell. We're dying to know," Marina chimed in.

The ladies continued to gush over each other's attire and jewelry. *How appropriate Laura should be wearing red*, Sylvia thought.

"May I interest you in a cocktail?" asked the waiter, much to the relief of the men, who had been standing by waiting patiently for the ladies to finish their apparent mutual admiration.

"Yes, let's all have a cocktail, and let the celebration begin," proclaimed Brian rubbing his hands together.

The cocktails arrived and the conversation flowed as everyone appeared genuinely excited by the occasion and being on board ship. Both Sylvia and David momentarily forgot their heartaches and moved with the moment. They started to adjourn to the dinner table as Robin and Jill finally arrived.

"I am so sorry we're late, Mother," Robin puffed, looking embarrassed. He knew how his mother detested unpunctuality.

"That's quite all right," Sylvia said soothingly. She was not about to let their bad form ruin her evening.

"Oh Sylvia, you look lovely," Jill said admiringly.

"Why thank you, Jill. And your dress is so ..." Sylvia was at a loss for words, as she looked at the tight fitting white bodice and bright, multi-colored silk skirt with its loud abstract art design. Sylvia found her voice. "…. unique. So perfectly unique," she finished.

Jill raised the one side of her dress with her hand revealing large orange and yellow circles linked to bright blue squares with scarlet triangles. "I'm so glad you like it. I was terrified you wouldn't."

"Why, I'm flattered you consider my opinion so valuable. Shall we go in?"

Sylvia directed everyone to their seats.

"Wow, look at all these knives and forks. How will I know which one to use?" Jill was overwhelmed.

"You just start from the outside and work your way to the centre. It's really quite simple, my dear. I'm sure you can figure it out." Both Brian and Robin scowled at Sylvia. She immediately wished she could retract her sarcastic comment. Fortunately, the steward arrived at the table and approached Brian.

"Good evening, Mr. Sinclair. Welcome aboard.

My name is Maurizio. I will be taking care of you and your guests for the duration of your journey across the Atlantic."

"Say, haven't I seen you somewhere before?" Brian inquired, trying to place the face. "You look vaguely familiar."

"I would doubt that Mr. Sinclair."

"Where were you before working here?"

"I worked at the Hotel Daniele in Venice."

"And before that?"

"I've always worked at the Hotel Daniele."

"Strange, you don't sound Italian."

"My parents are American, but I was born and raised in Italy. May I start pouring the champagne, Sir?"

Brian nodded. Maurizio popped the cork, rounded the table and filled the guest's glasses.

Marshall stood up, glass in hand, which he tapped with a spoon to draw everyone's attention. "Having known the hosts longer than anyone else, except for Marina," he acknowledged, "I feel I am entitled to the distinct privilege of making the toast to give thanks and to honor our hosts, Brian and Sylvia." He looked toward Sylvia. "Sylvia, you are as beautiful as the day I first met you all those years ago. You are the very personification of charm, grace, and elegance. As a friend of the family, I love you now as much as I loved you then."

"Why, you never told me I had competition, sweetheart?" Brian guffawed.

"My good friend, Brian. I thank you for your friendship, the confidence you have placed in me, and for always considering me part of your family. I'm sure I speak for everyone here, when I thank you for hosting this magnificent celebration and for including us all. We all wish you many, many more years of marital bliss and hope we are all here for your golden anniversary." Laura cast her eyes downward, feeling a pang of guilt as she reached for David's hand. Everyone else laughed heartily enjoying the mirth and merriment of the moment.

"I ask you to raise your glass to Sylvia and Brian." Everyone stood and raised their glasses. "To Sylvia and Brian," they said in unison as they sipped their champagne and applauded the couple.

The conversation around the table started to flow.

Stephanie reached across for her mother's hand. "I'm so happy for you, Mother. I really am. And you look so beautiful this evening," she said tenderly.

"Thank you, dear. And now what was the news you had that you mentioned over the telephone when I was in London?"

"Oh, I'll tell you when the time is right. I know your actual anniversary is not until the end of the week, but tonight belongs to you and Dad.

Maurizio arrived at the table, and handed everyone menus.

"What a truly magnificent meal," Brian exclaimed, patting his stomach. "Honey, do you have my blood pressure pills?"

Maurizio was rounding the table with the large silver coffee pot topping everyone's cup, as Sylvia fumbled in her purse. She found the container and passed it down the table.

"Sylvia, what a delightful little pill box," Laura noted as she observed the ornate design. "Wherever did you find it?"

Sylvia's mind returned to the day she acquired it, when her intent was to purchase some tablets to help Laura. Rage surged inside, but she maintained her composure.

"I bought it at Harrods when I was there. They were selling them at the counter in the pharmacy. I am sure you can purchase one at the Harrods gift shop on board ship. They're sure to have them, especially with the number of people who will undoubtedly be suffering from motion sickness." She chuckled at her own joke.

"I guess we should be heading to the showroom" said Brian, looking at his watch, and swallowing his pill.

"I must say, it's all rather mysterious as to who the entertainer will be," commented David. "I mean, fancy announcing on the marquee that it is to be a surprise international singing star. Are you giving us one of your cabaret performances, Todd, you sly devil?"

Laura bumped her husband's side, knowing that Todd had not had a gig in ages.

"I should be so lucky," responded Todd drily as he took another swig of his whiskey.

There was a slight uncomfortable pause.

"You're right, Brian. We really should make a move," interjected Marina.

They all departed the dining room and headed toward

the showroom chatting gaily as they went. They were shown to their long reserved table at the side of the dance floor below the stage.

Backstage, Denise Parker was looking at herself in the mirror. What she saw was a beautiful woman in a tight fitting royal blue sequined evening dress accentuating a trim figure and highlighting a still full bosom. "You look great. Now go out and knock 'em dead," she said to the mirror, knowing she would 'wow' her audience. She made her way from her dressing room and gingerly peeked through the curtains to see if she could spot her targets. She saw Brian and Sylvia and their party making their way across the dance floor to their seats. No sooner were they all settled and dinner liqueurs brought to the table when the lights dimmed. In the center of the room the mirrored disco ball started rotating slowly, spreading its rays across the room as it twirled.

There was a forceful drum roll as the audience started to quiet down. In a deep voice, the compère announced, "Ladies and Gentleman, Cunard, the world's most luxurious shipping line, has the enormous pleasure and privilege to present one of the world's greatest and truly legendary talents. She is an international recording star, television star, and cabaret artiste. Please put your hands together and welcome the incomparable, the fabulous, the one and only Denise Parker!" The orchestra burst into the chorus of one of Denise's most famous hits, as the curtains drew back. The audience applauded with great gusto, as she grabbed the microphone, took a quick bow and moved down from the stage onto the dance floor basking in the thunderous applause.

She immediately burst into song and started to work her magic seduction of the audience, knowing that she fully intended to let Brian see what he had spurned almost twenty six years ago.

Brian was speechless. His jaw dropped in amazement, while Sylvia was aghast as her face turned ashen. She wanted to leave, and immediately started to rise from her seat, but Marina, who was sitting next to her, grabbed her friend's arm firmly, and held her down. She knew if Sylvia left, it would have exacerbated a potentially explosive situation. Laura shot a glance across the table toward Sylvia. *How in the world did this happen, and what was Denise up to?* she wondered. She was now feeling very guilty for having betrayed her good friend and was equally as angry at Brian for having engaged in their trysts. Like Laura, Marshall wondered why Denise had chosen this cruise and was wary of what might lay ahead. Alicia was so startled she dropped her liqueur glass on the floor, and tried in vain to see if her dress was stained. Stephanie, Jean- Louis and Robin were all indifferent, oblivious to the dynamics of the situation, while Jill whistled her approval vociferously. "Gee, she's one of my all time favorites. I just can't believe it. I wonder if I can get her autograph later."

Todd and David wondered whether Denise would recognize them in the audience, and invite them onto the stage for a duet.

Denise continued to bounce around the dance floor engaging her audience with her well known and crowd pleasing hits, and a few love ballads. She dazzled her audience for almost an hour before slowly moving toward the Sinclair table. "Ladies and Gentlemen," she purred. "May I introduce you to a man to whom I owe my career — and so much more," she added teasingly and suggestively, "Mr. Brian Sinclair." The spotlight fell on Brian, who stood and bowed slightly as the audience applauded loudly. He was slightly embarrassed. Denise kissed him softly on the cheek. Sylvia had had enough. She started to rise. Denise continued, "And please welcome his charming and delightful wife, Mrs. Sylvia Sinclair." The spotlight fell on Sylvia. Startled, she smiled feebly, nodded and sat down again. *What* is *she up to, the conniving witch?* Sylvia thought.

Denise was in her glory. "The Sinclairs are celebrating their silver wedding anniversary. Isn't that fabulous?" The audience clapped loudly.

"And now, I'd like to complete my show tonight with one of my all time favorite songs, made famous by Miss Doris Day."

As she stood in front of Brian, looking at him, she started to sing "I'll Never Stop Loving You."

My God, it's as if she's seducing him, Laura thought.

Poor Sylvia, Marina empathized as she looked at her friend's face.

Sylvia remained stoic. An ominous feeling pervaded the table, as the not so subtle nuance was not lost on most of the people sitting there.

The song finished. "Thank you. I love you and goodnight." Denise blew kisses to the audience and made her way backstage, the curtains drawing behind her. There were shouts of "Bravo," "More," and "Encore" from the audience, but Denise continued to her dressing room. She kicked her shoes off, lit up a cigarette, poured herself some champagne and looked at herself in the mirror again. *You did it gal!* she said to herself.

There was a sudden knock at the door. *Well I wonder who that is*, she thought. She walked to the door and opened it.

"Well, well, well. This is a surprise. I certainly never expected to see you here." She eyed her visitor up and down. "Would you like to join me in a glass of champagne?" Denise opened her door wide, and gestured for her guest to enter.

CHAPTER 11

Alicia stepped into the dressing room with great trepidation. She and Denise had never been friends.

"Well, I must say, it was a surprise for me to see you with the Sinclairs tonight. How in the world did your paths cross?" Denise asked curiously.

"I married a wealthy financier."

"Yes, I remember reading that in the newspaper. You really moved into high society," Denise mocked.

"Bruce and I played tennis at the country club and we met Brian on the court." Alicia spoke softly and with apprehension. "Then we started playing bridge with Sylvia and Brian and over the years became close friends. Then of course, Bruce died." She sat down.

"I'm sorry," Denise commented unconvincingly. "Did you ever tell Brian about your affair with Greg Calderman when he was with Sinclair records? Did you tell him you were pregnant with Greg's child and almost wrecked his marriage?"

"I never knew you were so cold Denise, until now. Of course I didn't tell Brian," she snapped. "Neither he nor Sylvia is aware I even knew Greg. Nobody knew, except for you. Bruce didn't even know. Why Greg ever even told you is a total mystery to me. There was no reason for him to divulge such information."

"Poor, poor Alicia," Denise sneered. "Of course Greg confided in me. When Brian threw me over for Sylvia, I turned to Greg. He understood. He was my best friend, and helped me get through a very hard and difficult time." Reading Alicia's mind, she continued, "No, we were never lovers, but he was like a brother to me, and I like a sister to him." She crossed her leg on her knee, and started to massage her toes. "When you became pregnant with his child he didn't know what to do. He was very much in love with his wife. He couldn't tell her, so naturally he discussed it with me. He knew I'd keep it to myself."

"You think I don't know he loved his wife?" Alicia started to get angry. "He was the one who insisted I have an abortion. I've had to live with that every day. I was the one who was devastated. Greg was the only man I ever truly loved. I wanted his child so much. Then, when he committed suicide, I was alone, and scared and frightened. I was so young. I had no one. I had the procedure alone." She sobbed a little as the haunting memories of her past resurfaced. "But Bruce understood. He was much older, but he was the kindest, gentlest man I ever met. He was safe and secure, and loved me dearly. I think he knew in his heart that although I loved him, I wasn't in love with him, but he accepted it anyway. He never questioned my past."

Denise was unmoved. She lit another cigarette, and poured herself some more champagne. "You could have at least attended Greg's funeral and paid your final respects."

Alicia pulled herself together. "Don't be absurd. How on earth could I have gone to his funeral? I was pregnant. I hadn't even had the operation at that time. I was still dealing with the decision to have an abortion, and then I had to face a life without Greg. I wouldn't have been able to look Terri in the face."

"Oh please! Don't tell me you actually have a conscience?"

The two women looked at each other with contempt. There was no love lost between them. The uneasy silence was palpable.

Denise continued. "So, you obviously still believe Greg committed suicide?"

Alicia was shocked at the question. "Well, I always thought it seemed out of character, but that's what all the reports said. Surely you're not suggesting otherwise?" She was bewildered. "Are you saying he was murdered? But, by whom? Who would have done such a thing? What a preposterous suggestion!"

"Is it? Well, what do you think? Greg was as honest as the day is long. There is no way he would have embezzled from the company. No, Brian and Marshall made it look like Greg had embezzled from the company."

"But why? Why would they do such a thing? I just don't believe it."

"Oh Alicia, could you really have been that naïve?" She stared at Alicia. "Of course! Greg would never have bothered you with mundane things like the truth. Marshall and Brian wanted Greg to falsify their government tax returns to reduce their heavy tax liability. Greg wouldn't go along with their game, so they tried to buy him out. Greg wouldn't budge. They just outmaneuvered him. Greg threatened to go to the government, and guess what? They dispensed with him."

Alicia sat there dumbfounded. "I can't believe it. I

simply can't believe it," she repeated. "Brian and Marshall are not capable of such a thing. Besides, even if they did and if you knew, why didn't *you* do something about it at the time?"

"Who would believe us? Neither Terri nor I had positive proof. Besides, we were scared. That's why as soon as the funeral was over, Terri hightailed it off to Europe. But I saw Greg the night before his death. No way was he going to commit suicide."

"Are you still in touch with Terri? How is she doing?"

"Haven't a clue. Haven't seen or heard from her since the day of the funeral. She knew what I knew. But she was frightened for her life. She told me she would be leaving and wouldn't be contacting me. Terri didn't want anyone to know where she was going. Anyway, why should you care? You never cared for her before, otherwise you wouldn't have slept with her husband. You certainly wouldn't have gotten yourself pregnant."

Alicia stood up. "That was a despicable thing to say, Denise. No wonder Brian dumped you for Sylvia. She has more class than you'll ever have." She turned and headed toward the door.

"You're hardly one to talk about class," Denise scoffed. "See you around, kiddo."

Alicia slammed the door as she left. Denise poured herself another drink. Who would have thought their paths would cross again after all these years? Now she could really put the cat among the pigeons if she wanted, although she probably had already, she mused. *What a bonus surprise* she thought.

Alicia made her way back to her cabin. She was not

of the mind to return to the party. She would make her apologies to her hosts the next day. As she readied herself for bed, she reflected on her conversation with Denise Parker. If what Denise had told her was true, how could she face Marshall and Brian again? How could she sit with them, eat with them, be with them, for the next five days? Marshall would never have acted alone. Brian would have had to have instigated it. Could it really be possible Brian was responsible for the death of the only man she had ever truly loved? Even though nothing could ever have come of her romance with Greg, Brian had cut short her relationship. She would never forgive him for that.

Back in the showroom, the passengers were beginning to dance to the orchestra, as an air of festivity pervaded the room. At the Sinclair table, it was slightly different.

Stephanie noticed the look of anguish on her mother's face. "Are you all right, Mother?" She touched her mother's arm tenderly.

"Actually, I have quite a headache. Brian, will you take me back to our cabin please?" She placed her hand over her forehead.

"Sure thing, honey." Brian was not looking forward to the rest of the evening.

"Todd, it's been a long day. Why don't we turn in too?" Marina empathized with her friend, and the evening had lost its luster.

Todd shrugged. "I think Denise Parker could have at least introduced us, too. Don't you agree, David?"

David nodded in agreement. "Yes, I thought she should have asked us to at least sing one number with her. She had to have recognized us."

"I can't believe your egos." Laura pulled at her husband. "Come on, let's go to bed."

"Where's Alicia? I'll escort her back to her room." Marshall looked around the table.

"Oh, she accidentally spilled her drink during the show. She was going to her room to see if her dress was stained, and then try and remove it," Stephanie replied.

"Do you think we could see if we could get Denise Parker's autograph?" Jill was still mesmerized from the show.

"I don't think so," Robin replied wearily.

"Well, can we dance then?"

"No. Let's just call it a night and go to bed like all the others, shall we?"

Jill began to pout. Robin knew something was awry with his mother and dad, but was not of a mind to pursue it.

"Maybe we'll see you all at breakfast. If not, it's lunch at twelve thirty," Sylvia informed her guests, as she and Brian departed.

They all headed back toward their cabins, somewhat subdued.

Behind all the others, Stephanie whispered softly to Jean-Louis. "Something has just happened. I'm not sure what, but it has something to do with Denise Parker."

Jean-Louis was perplexed. "Everything is fine. You're imagining things."

Stephanie contradicted him. "You're wrong. I know

my mother. I hope the trip is not ruined for her."

"Nonsense. Your mother is fine. She just had a headache."

Stephanie shook her head at her husband. Just like him. *Just like a man*, she thought, *totally clueless.*

Once inside their suite, Brian pre-empted his wife. "Don't start, Sylvia. I had nothing to do with it. I don't know why Denise Parker is here. It was a total surprise to me."

"What the hell is she doing here?" Sylvia fumed. "Who tipped her off?" She'd totally forgotten Brian had broadcast to the world on the TV show a few months earlier of their silver wedding anniversary plans. "I'll bet she's the one who has the suite next door to us. I've a good mind to knock on the door to find out. If it is her, I'll give her a piece of my mind."

Brian knew that wouldn't happen. His wife was not confrontational.

"Honey, don't let Denise Parker ruin our special anniversary. Whatever her game is, nobody's playing. What do you want me to do? You know how much I love you." *I wish I knew that for sure*, Sylvia thought as she wondered whether now would be the time to tell Brian she was aware of his tryst with Laura in London. As she undressed, she thought better of it, unsure of where the conversation might lead.

Brian sat quietly on the side of the bed. He knew how much time and effort Sylvia had put into the planning of the trip and felt badly for her. He wondered who in the group was still in contact with his former fiancée. He waited for Sylvia to finish in the bathroom before he changed into his silk pajamas. He really wanted to go to the bar for a drink or play at the casino, anywhere to remove himself from the unpleasant atmosphere now surrounding him, but knew the merest suggestion would just add fuel to the fire. Without saying anymore he climbed into bed beside his wife, turned out the light, and fell asleep almost immediately. As the moonlight shone through the gap in the drapes, Sylvia lay restless looking at Brian's back, knowing she would hardly sleep a wink.

CHAPTER 12

Sylvia was the first one to arrive at the breakfast table. She had hardly slept all night, but was determined not to let the events of the previous evening mar her anniversary celebration even further. Denise Parker was an unexpected shock, but she was now prepared, and Denise would not be able to catch her off balance again. Being first at the table was a statement to the others that she was in control.

Marshall was soon to join her. On his way to the table, he saw Maurizio and pulled him to one side. "Here's fifty bucks. Get me the cabin number of Denise Parker." Maurizio nodded discreetly.

Before he could say anything to Sylvia, she commented, "Isn't it a beautiful morning? There's such a soft gentle breeze. What do you plan on doing today?"

Sylvia obviously was not willing to discuss what had transpired the previous night. Marshall picked up on the cue. "I hope your headache has gone?"

Sylvia nodded. Marshall paused. "I think I'll just take this morning and explore the ship. She clearly is a beauty."

Marina and Todd arrived in the dining room with Laura and David. Both Laura and Marina had instructed their spouses not to mention Denise Parker in front of Sylvia. The husbands were baffled, but acquiesced to the wishes of their wives.

"Sylvia, isn't it a super day? What's on the agenda?" Marina chirped.

"I thought I would visit the spa and salon to see what's there. Care to join me?"

"Absolutely," said Marina. "I'll bet it's divine."

"Count me in. Didn't have time to go before I left," added Laura. She knew this was the time to stand by her friend. Hopefully too, she was proving to David that she was trying to make amends, and maybe salvage her own marriage.

Brian came bounding in and joined everyone at the table.

"Coffee, please, Maurizio, and just some toast. What's happening?"

Sylvia sipped her own coffee. "We were just discussing our plans for the morning. We ladies are going to the spa and salon. Marshall's going to tour the ship and advise us what's worth seeing, aren't you Marshall?" She turned to David. "What about you?"

"I imagine I'll check out the library. I understand they have a good selection. I love to read, and somehow, at home, I never seem to find the time for it," David replied.

"Since you are going to the spa, honey, I think I'll visit the gym. See if they have some good workout equipment. Have to keep this body of mine in shape you know." Brian flexed his muscles.

"Think I'll join you." Todd thought it would be a great opportunity to get Brian alone and discuss his contract renewal. Brian groaned to himself.

"I wonder what has happened to Alicia?" Sylvia inquired. "Maybe we should knock on her door and see if she wants to join us at the salon?"

"Oh honey, I forgot to tell you. Alicia called just after you left. She sounded a little out of sorts. She said she was still tired, probably due to the sea air, and would join us for lunch. I told her lunch was twelve thirty."

"Well, it doesn't look like the kids are going to join us for breakfast either. I think I'll pop back to the suite and meet you ladies at the salon at, let's say, ten o'clock?" Sylvia prepared to leave the table as Laura and Marina agreed to the time.

Brian finished his toast. "I'll come with you, dear."

The others chatted at the table for a while and then departed, leaving Marshall by himself.

As soon as everyone had left, Maurizio approached Marshall. "Sir, Ms. Denise Parker is occupying the Queen Elizabeth Suite across from Mr. and Mrs. Sinclair."

"Thank you, Maurizio," Marshall responded. An ominous feeling overcame him. He returned to his cabin.

⁂

Brian was pounding away on the exercise bike, when he saw Todd enter the gym.

"Mind if I join you?" Todd asked.

"Be my guest."

Todd straddled the neighboring bicycle and started to pedal. He was not used to working out and was clumsy. He was puffing and panting heavily.

"Long time since you and I have had a chat alone, Brian," he offered gingerly.

"Stop beating around the bush, Todd. What's on your

mind?" Brian looked straight ahead and kept his focus on his bicycle.

"Well, I was hoping to talk about my contract, which is …"

Brian cut him off. "Contracts are not my department. Marshall handles and signs all the recording contracts."

"Yes, but Marshall has said he has prepared and signed the contract and it is on your desk for review. He said it's been sitting there for quite a while now."

"I'll look at it in due course."

"Well, when will that be?"

Brian was irritated. "When I am good and ready, Todd." He stopped pedaling his bicycle. "Frankly, Todd, from what I've read, I think Marshall's contract is too generous. I don't know what he's thinking. Look at you. You're a mess — and that's when you're sober. And you're not sober even half the time. I can't get you concert bookings anymore, and when did you last have a hit record?"

Todd fought back. "I was your number one recording star for many years, Brian. You and Sinclair Records made a ton of dough through me and my talent." He got off the bike and moved toward Brian.

"That was a long time ago, Todd, a very long time ago. I think we've settled that score with the royalties and annual fees we've been paying you over the years. Now, if you'll excuse me." Brian grabbed his towel and headed toward the shower.

Todd wondered what he would have to do to get the contract off Brian's desk and get his own signature on it alongside Marshall's. He resented Brian and his cocky attitude.

Marshall heard Brian saying goodbye to Sylvia outside their suite and the three ladies chatting as they headed past his cabin toward the spa. A few moments later, he heard Stephanie and Jean-Louis leave their cabin. It sounded like they were heading toward the pool. Once the voices were out of hearing range, he walked along the corridor and knocked on Denise Parker's door.

"Well if it isn't my old buddy, Marshall Thornton. I was wondering when you would come barreling along," Denise scoffed.

"Cut it out, Denise. What the hell do you think you're playing at?" he responded, entering her suite. She closed the door behind him.

"I'm not playing at anything, Buster. I'm earning my living." Denise was not about to be intimidated. She was not the immature young rising star Marshall knew all those years ago.

"You don't fool me. You're up to something. If you so much as ruin this event for Sylvia ..."

"Why, you're *still* in love with that broad after all these years, aren't you?" she mocked.

"Shut up, Denise. I'm warning you, if you do anything to disrupt this celebration, you'll be sorry. That was quite a little display of affection you showed last night."

Denise walked toward Marshall until she was almost touching him, and even though she was much shorter than he, she stared him straight in the eye.

"Don't you dare threaten me, Marshall Thornton! Don't think for one minute that show was for real. I loathe and detest that despicable little man. He's responsible for the death of my best friend. Don't think I don't know what happened with Greg Calderman twenty odd years ago."

"Are you threatening me?"

"Cut the crap, Marshall. I know what you did to Greg in cahoots with Mr. Brian smarty-pants Sinclair. Things are different now. I have bodyguards, I have money and I have fame. Don't think I won't use them if you so much as even try to lay a finger on me. So just get your sorry ass out of my suite, before I call security." She stormed to the door and opened it.

"This is not the end of this discussion, Denise. Believe me, you can be sure of that," Marshall warned as he left her suite.

She closed the door behind him. *How dare he come and try and steamroll me,* she fumed. She wondered whether Brian had put Marshall up to it. *Would be just like that miserable coward to get someone else to do his dirty work.* She ordered a late breakfast from the cabin service and decided to go to the spa after she had finished. A nice little facial would do the trick. She calmed herself down at the prospect of the luxury of a facial massage and called to make the appointment.

"I can strongly recommend the body massage," said Sylvia. "It was heavenly."

"My facial treatment was simply fabulous. One of the best I've ever had," Marina purred.

"You haven't had anything until you have the manicure

and pedicure. They say that a pedicure is the second best thing to sex. If you ask me it's better," joked Laura, before realizing how inappropriate her remark was.

They all laughed as they turned to leave the salon. They stopped short as they ran into Denise entering the spa for her facial.

"Denise," nodded Sylvia in a clipped tone.

"Well, if it isn't Sylvia Sinclair. Aren't you going to thank me for the lovely tribute I gave you last night?"

"Glad your career is doing so well, Denise. What a shame you couldn't find a husband along the way," Sylvia lamented sarcastically.

"Well, you might just want to be a little careful. Maybe I'll steal yours away."

Marina intercepted. "Come on, Sylvia. Let's go. It's almost lunchtime."

Denise turned her scorn toward Marina. "And Marina, dear, just how is that lush of a husband of yours? He didn't look too good when I saw him last night. I would have asked him to sing a duet with me, but I didn't know if he could stand on his own two feet for two minutes."

It was Laura's turn.

"Denise Parker, no wonder you never found a husband. You've probably never slept with anybody. I don't know how you can even sleep with yourself, much less get anyone else to sleep with you."

"Maybe you just want to check with your own husband, Laura, darling. Perhaps I slept with him," she taunted, brushing them aside. "I'm sure we'll all be seeing a lot of each other on the cruise, so if you'll excuse me. I see you've all had your much needed treatments, now I have an appointment for my facial." She waved to them as she continued into the spa.

"I'll alert the beauticians to have a knife ready to scrape off all the layers," Laura shot back, as she, Sylvia and Marina left.

"We missed you this morning, Alicia," Sylvia said welcoming her friend to the lunch table.

"So sorry, Sylvia, I was just so tired. I don't know why." She noticed everyone was seated in the same chairs as the prior evening, and sat down in her previously assigned position.

"They have bridge this afternoon according to the activities board. Anyone interested in playing?" Sylvia asked.

"Deal me in," said Alicia. "I haven't played for quite a while though."

"I'll join you," said Marshall.

Alicia suddenly felt uncomfortable in the presence of Marshall and Brian. Denise Parker was convincing, yet devious. Could she trust Denise's word? Alicia was going to have to figure out how to find the truth.

"I think I'll have a nice quiet afternoon nap," said Jill. She kicked off her shoe and ran her foot slowly and gently up Brian's leg. He was immediately aroused, and looked at Jill. Could she be serious? She continued to massage Brian's legs as she licked her lips. "It seems the perfect afternoon to just lie naked, well, almost naked on my bed," she continued, giggling.

Sylvia was appalled by the comment but chose to ignore it, turning her attention to Brian. "How about you, dear, will you come and play?"

"I think I'll pass this afternoon. I may have overdone it in the gym. I think I'll take a nap also," Brian replied. "What do you plan to do, Robin?" he deflected.

"I'm going to try my hand in the casino. I'm feeling quite lucky."

"Jean-Louis and I are going to look at all the shops," Stephanie contributed, relieved that Jill was having a nap and didn't ask to join her on her shopping expedition.

"Todd and I thought we'd just lie by the pool. It seems such a lovely afternoon. Would you and David like to join us?" Marina asked.

"Sure. That sounds like fun, doesn't it, David?" Laura looked at her husband.

"Whatever makes you happy," David responded drily.

"Well it seems like everyone is going to have an interesting time. Will look forward to hearing about everyone's day at dinner tonight," Sylvia concluded.

Brian moved his leg away from Jill, to see if her foot would follow. He wanted to be sure he was receiving the right message. Sure enough, Jill's foot ventured over to his ankle. *I'm not sure you'll hear about mine*, Brian thought as he once again noted Jill's ample bosom heaving alongside him as she showed it off to maximum effect. She was still rubbing her foot up and down his leg.

CHAPTER 13

As everyone was finishing their lunch, Stephanie decided it was a good time to reveal her news.

"Mother, Dad, I have an announcement to make. Jean-Louis and I have some wonderful news to share with you. You're going to be grand-parents. Happy Anniversary."

"Darling, that's wonderful!" Sylvia embraced her daughter and shed a tear of excitement. She turned and grabbed Jean-Louis' hand and hugged him. "Brian, isn't it wonderful? Isn't that just the best anniversary gift?"

Brian looked doleful. "Well, I was rather hoping our first grandchild would have the name Sinclair," he lamented.

Sylvia angrily shot him a look of disgust. There were times she could not believe his selfishness and insensitivity.

Defusing what she saw as an uncomfortable situation brewing, Marina jumped in. "How very exciting for you both," she enthused, remembering herself when Robin and Stephanie were born. The others all chimed in with their congratulations and questions. "When is the baby due?" "Is it a girl or a boy?" were repeated questions.

"I hope if the baby is a girl, you will name her after me!" Jill twittered, as Stephanie raised her eyes.

"Congratulations, Sis," Robin offered begrudgingly.

Jean-Louis was repelled by his father-in-law's comments. *How I despise that man*, he thought before apologizing to Sylvia. "Please excuse me, I think I will get some fresh air." He left the table and headed onto the deck, glaring down at the water churning below. He was soon joined by Brian, who stood alongside, looking at the horizon.

"Okay, what is it going to take for you to leave this family?"

Jean-Louis turned and stared at his father-in-law. "What?" he asked incredulously.

"How much do you want? I want you out of our family and out of my daughter's life," Brian continued, still staring straight ahead and not looking at his son-in-law.

"You really are a cold, hard-hearted, bastard, Brian!"

"You will never amount to anything. You can't even support Stephanie. How are you going to support a kid?"

"We do just fine now. We'll be fine too, when the baby is born."

"Unless you leave Stephanie, or Stephanie gets rid of the baby, don't either of you come looking to me for financial support," Brian threatened.

Jean-Louis was ready to punch him. He stared at Brian contemptuously.

"I have no intentions of leaving Stephanie and we plan to have the baby, whether you like it or not," he said, gritting his teeth. "And we don't want or need any of your damn money."

"Well, let's see what Stephanie has to say about that. If she stays with you and keeps the baby, as soon as I get back to the States, I'll have her removed as beneficiary from my estate."

"You're sick, Brian. You really are a sick man."

Brian finally turned, and looked Jean-Louis in the face. "What's your game? What are you up to? I've had my private eye check you out. They can't find anything on you. But I know you are up to something."

"I just happen to love your daughter. Is that so hard to understand?" He returned to the restaurant just as everyone was leaving their seats. Brian followed him inside.

"Darling, let me escort you to the bridge room." Brian took Sylvia's arm. Marshall and Alicia followed them, Alicia still feeling uncomfortable and preoccupied. She wished she'd waited until she heard Marshall's plans for the afternoon before committing herself to bridge. She was now feeling more repelled by Brian. His indifference toward his new grandchild was not lost on her.

Sylvia scolded Brian as they walked along the corridor, and pulled her arm away from his. "How could you be so cruel to Stephanie and Jean-Louis? Your own daughter. Your own grand-child!"

"Sorry, darling. You're right. It was a bit thoughtless of me," he placated.

A middle-aged man was seated by himself in the bridge room and Sylvia invited him to make up a foursome.

"Name's Richard, Richard Manning," said the guest, shaking hands with Marshall.

"And what do you do for a living, Mr. Manning?" asked Marshall, as Sylvia dealt the cards.

"I'm a retired private eye. Criminal investigations," said Richard, matter-of-factly, all the while looking at the expressions on the faces of the players at the table.

"How interesting. I imagine you have some wonderfully

exciting escapades to share. One heart," bid Sylvia. She studied the face of her bridge partner. What a seemingly unassuming individual. *If he was on 'What's My Line' I'd never have guessed him to be a private eye*, she thought. His slightly receding hair line, knitted brows, and strong, protruding jaw line gave him an intriguing face, and she looked forward to the afternoon with this interesting character and, hopefully, to hearing some of his stories.

Having watched them settle down to their first round of bridge, Brian headed to the deck overlooking the swimming pool. He saw Marina, Todd, Laura and David laying down their towels and rubbing themselves and each other with their suntan lotion. He hurried along to the casino and observed Robin at the roulette table.

"Here's five hundred bucks for you to bet for me. Make sure you win me some money!" He slapped his hands on his son's shoulder.

"Will do my best, Dad," Robin replied enthusiastically. He loved the sound of the roulette wheel.

"*Rien ne va plus*," ordered the croupier, as Brian headed off. As he saw Stephanie and Jean-Louis staring in the shop windows below, he sprinted to Jill's cabin.

Inside her cabin, he eyed her with a mixture of lasciviousness and suspicion, as she stood before him in her brief negligee, a seductive look on her face.

"What the hell are you up to? What do you want from me?"

Jill moved toward her bed and lay down slowly parting her negligee. *Gone is the giggling and immature Jill*, Brian thought, as he feasted his eyes upon the body that lay before him.

"I want a man, not a boy. I want a real man," she panted, as she licked her lips, and slowly ran her fingers through her hair, beckoning him toward her with her eyes.

Brian moved forward slowly removing his jacket. He climbed on top of her and began caressing her breasts sensuously and voraciously with his hands and his mouth, as Jill started to writhe in ecstasy.

Brian lay exhausted, realizing he was not as youthful as he once was. Still he appeared to satisfy Jill's seemingly insatiable appetite. He arose and started to dress himself.

"Same time tomorrow?" Jill asked as she basked in the joy of their compatibility.

"Not a chance."

"Why not? I bet I'm the best lay you've ever had." She got up off her bed, stunned by his rebuke.

Brian shrugged. "You're an O.K. lay. But you're my son's girlfriend."

Jill was furious. She turned on him. "That didn't bother you before. You can't use me like this."

"I have, and I did."

"Oh yes? And what do you think Robin will say when I tell him? And what about Sylvia?" Jill was truly scorned, and vengeful.

"Nothing. Because you're not going to tell him, you little slut."

Jill raised her hand to slap him. He grabbed it.

"And you're not going to say anything to my wife either. Because I had you checked out by a private eye before you even stepped foot on this trip. I know full well about your past and how, as a juvenile back in Philadelphia, you shot your step-father."

"That bastard raped me," Jill cried. "He had it coming to him."

"He may have. But, you're not going to blackmail me. You're fine as long as you are Robin's floozy, but I'll tell him about your past if there is any indication he plans to make you a part of this family."

He pushed her back on the bed and slammed the door behind him as he made his way back to his cabin.

Jill lay on her bed sobbing. A few minutes later, she heard the key in the lock of her cabin. "My God, it's Robin," she said quietly. She darted to the bathroom to clean her face and freshen up.

"Hey, sexy, where are you?"

"I'm in the bathroom, Robin. I'll be right out." She emerged wearing a robe and fluffing her hair. "You're back from the casino early."

"Well, I wasn't as lucky as I hoped. Maybe I'd have better luck with you by my side."

He grabbed her, and started to kiss her on the cheek. She pushed him away. "Not now, honey."

"What do you mean, 'not now'?"

"I'm not in the mood."

Robin grabbed her again, and spun her around throwing her on the bed. "You're always in the mood." He fell on top of her, and parted her robe.

"No, please, no!" Jill cried out.

"I'll soon have you in the mood," Robin teased as he

excitedly nestled his face in her breasts, ignoring her protests.

Suddenly, he pulled himself back. "My God, I smell cologne. That's my father's cologne. My God! My father's been here hasn't he?" he said in disbelief. He got up from the bed, and wiped his mouth. He could almost taste the cologne.

"That's my father's brand. It's a special blend. I can smell it. It's not the cologne you buy in a regular department store."

Jill had never seen Robin this angry. She was stunned and knowing she was trapped, couldn't deny it. Not knowing what to say, she mumbled a feeble, "I love you, Robin." She arose from the bed, closed her robe, and moved timidly toward him.

"Get away from me, you whore!" He slapped her across the face and she fell back onto the bed. She screamed from the pain, and started to cry uncontrollably into the pillow.

Robin ran from her cabin and out onto the deck. He clutched onto the railings, looking out to sea. He was so angry he could barely see straight.

"Are you all right, Robin?"

Robin was startled. He spun around to see David walking toward him.

"Oh, hi David. Yes, I'm fine thanks. Had enough of the pool already?" he stumbled.

"No, I've just come up to get an aspirin for Laura. She has a slight headache. Are you sure you're O.K? You look like you've seen a ghost." He was genuinely concerned.

Robin leaned forward and cast his head down between his hands, and started to cry.

"Hey guy, what is it?" David put his arm on the young man's shoulder.

Robin stammered. "I've got to tell someone. Its Dad … I've just found out Dad has been screwing *my* girlfriend … my own father. Can you imagine that? My own father is having sex with Jill. God, how I hate him! What a son of a bitch! I could just kill him!"

David could relate to that. The memory of when he discovered that Brian had sex with his wife in London came flooding back. He empathized with Robin's anguish and torment, as his own pain and anger resurfaced.

"What can I do? Please, don't tell anyone. I can't say anything to anyone," Robin continued despairingly. "I can't hurt Mother. If she ever found out … if she even had a suspicion, it would kill her."

Or more likely, if Sylvia found out, she would kill Brian, David mused.

"Don't worry. Your secret is safe with me," David reassured the young man as he thought of all the ramifications. He too, now despised Brian more than ever.

CHAPTER 14

Maurizio was circling the dinner table replenishing everyone's coffee cups.

"I'm so sorry Jill was unable to join us for dinner, Robin," Sylvia offered lamely as she ferreted through her purse for the pill box. It was time for Brian's blood pressure tablet again. She seemed triumphant when she finally retrieved it.

"Permit me, Mrs Sinclair." Maurizio placed the silver coffee pot on the nearby table, and offered his tray.

"Why, thank you, Maurizio." Sylvia put the box on his tray, and Maurizio walked alongside the table, placing it in front of Brian. Sylvia continued, "I do hope you will check in on Jill before you join us in the ballroom."

She was concerned the conversation at the dinner table seemed a little stilted. Brian seemed subdued, and clearly something was troubling both her children. As a mother, her intuitions toward her children were sound, and her protective instincts were never far from the surface.

Robin finished toying with his drink. "Sure thing, Mother. I'm heading off to see her now." He took a final gulp, banged the glass down, and left the table, huffily.

As always, Marina picked up on the uncomfortable atmosphere. "Come on everyone, I can hear the band playing in the ballroom. Let's dance the night away."

Laura concurred. "David, I hope you're wearing your Fred Astaire shoes this evening. I'm ready to trip the light fantastic."

They all arrived at the ballroom where the dance was in full swing. As they arrived at their reserved table, Brian ordered a round of drinks.

"Oh look, there's Richard Manning," declared a surprised Sylvia. She waved to him across the dance floor. He bowed his head slightly in acknowledgement.

"And look, there's Denise Parker — dancing with the Captain. Bet she's seated at the Captain's table," observed Laura.

"Yes. What a disagreeable surprise," sniffed Sylvia. They waited for the drinks to arrive. Sylvia soon switched her attention to the music as the band began playing "Misty," one of her favorite songs. "Darling, they're playing my song."

Brian led her to the dance floor, and they started swaying to the music, Sylvia resting her head on Brian's shoulder. Marshall accompanied Alicia onto the floor, followed by the other three couples.

"I must say you haven't seemed yourself today, Alicia. You seem pre-occupied. Are you all right?" he asked as they glided slowly round the dance floor.

Alicia was taken aback. "Everything's fine. You're imagining things," she lied.

"Oh, of course. I know. It can't be easy for you celebrating a wedding anniversary so soon after your own husband's passing. I'm sure you yearn for that love. I'm sorry."

She did yearn for that love, but it was not the love

Marshall was thinking. The cruise, her revealing conversation with Denise Parker, had revived many emotions and feelings she needed to confront. The scars with Greg had been re-opened. It was hard enough for her to have had to deal with Greg's suicide at the time, and now to have to deal with the possibility he was murdered was a lot for her to face. She wished she had never agreed to the cruise.

The song finished and everyone waited for the next tune to begin. The Captain escorted Denise Parker back to his table, and returned to the dance floor.

"Excuse me, Mr. Sinclair, may I have the pleasure of the next dance with Mrs. Sinclair?" Brian looked at his wife. Sylvia nodded, and put her hand on the Captain's shoulder as he took her other hand. Brian returned to his table and sat with his drink, watching his wife dancing very slowly with the Captain.

Denise maneuvered herself round the dance floor and quietly sidled onto the chair behind Brian. He did not notice her as he watched the dancers swaying in time to the music.

She sat for a few minutes observing Brian, the man whom she had once loved, and whom she now loathed, before whispering softly in his ear, "How about one dance for old time's sake?"

He was startled. "In God's name, what are you doing here? What are you up to, Denise?" He turned around to face her. "Why can't you leave us alone? What's your game?"

"My game? There's no 'game.' You've always thrived on excitement. I just thought I would add a little spice to your anniversary party. After all, we all go back such a long way, and I was most upset when I wasn't invited." Denise pouted with feigned petulance.

Marina observed Denise talking with Brian as she and Todd were moving around the dance floor. "We need to go back to the table. We can't let Sylvia see Brian talking to Denise."

"What's the big deal? Why is everyone hung up on Denise?" Todd was exasperated. Marina ignored him, and led him hastily back to the table.

"Why, Brian, aren't you going to ask me for a dance?" she interjected gaily, ignoring Denise.

Denise was clearly annoyed, and glared at Marina, who pulled Brian out of his chair and led him away. They disappeared into the center of the dance floor.

"I'd ask you for a dance, Todd Hammond, but you'd probably need another drink just to get around the floor," Denise said scornfully.

"I'd need more than another drink. I'd need another bottle before I'd dance with you, Denise," he fired back, and turned his face and attention back to the happenings on the dance floor. Irritated, Denise returned to her table, leaving Todd by himself.

Todd watched his wife dancing with Brian. *Brian really does have everything*, he thought enviously, and wondered more about how much longer he and Marina could afford their lifestyle and maintain their pretense.

"Thanks, Marina. I owe you one." Brian was relieved and genuinely thankful, as he led her masterfully in a quickstep.

"Well maybe it's payback time, now. I understand you

had a discussion this morning with Todd regarding his contract."

"Oh, please! Don't you start!" Brian pleaded. "In all honesty I can't renew his contract, Marina. Certainly not the one Marshall has prepared. I tell you what," he placated. "I promise I'll talk with Marshall when I get back to Los Angeles, and see what we can do. Now, can we let it go?"

Marina was unconvinced. She knew Brian was just brushing her off, and couldn't believe the husband of her best friend would treat her and Todd so shabbily. The song finished, and Brian saw Sylvia being escorted back. Thankful for the natural break, he led Marina back to her husband. Richard Manning arrived at the table, slightly ahead of the Captain and Sylvia. "May I have the pleasure of the next dance, Mrs Sinclair?"

She was surprised, but accepted the invitation to dance with the private investigator. "Why, thank you, Mr. Manning. I'd be delighted."

As they headed to mingle with the other dancers, they crossed paths with Jean-Louis and Stephanie leaving the floor.

"We have to sit this one out. Jean-Louis can't tango," laughed Stephanie.

"Why, Mr. Manning, you must meet my daughter." Sylvia introduced Stephanie and Jean-Louis to her bridge companion.

"Princess, how about a dance with your old man?" Brian joked as he stretched out his arms to the returning Stephanie, and glad not to have to sit with Todd and Marina.

"Sure, Dad."

The other couples exchanged partners and joined all the dancers on the now crowded ballroom floor, leaving Jean-Louis by himself. Contemptuously, he watched his father-in-law dance with his wife, unsure of how much longer he could maintain his façade. He couldn't wait for the cruise to end, and return to Sedona, and never have to deal with the Sinclair family ever again. He looked through the crowd on the floor for Sylvia. He would miss keeping in touch with her, but he reviled her husband. He would now have a reason to keep Stephanie all to himself.

"Princess, you don't look like you're having a good time. Aren't you enjoying yourself?" Brian asked of his daughter.

"Don't call me princess," she demanded.

"What are you so upset about?" Brian was genuinely mystified.

"Well, what do you think, Dad? Jean-Louis told me of your conversation after lunch today."

"That was man to man. He shouldn't have told you. But then, what would he know about 'man to man'?"

"You really are a pig, Dad. I don't know how or why Mother has put up with you all these years. And don't worry about cutting me out of the estate. I don't want anything from you, anyway. If we can't have your love, the last thing I want is your money." She broke away from her father and headed to the terrace, pleased she had got it off her chest.

Jean-Louis, who had been watching, promptly arose and followed his wife outside, knowing she probably had a disagreement with her father, which was what he was secretly hoping for. It meant she would turn to him more.

Brian shrugged and returned to the table. *I'll never understand that girl.*

He had no sooner sat down when Robin entered the ballroom accompanied by Jill, who was dressed in another gaudy outfit. They stood at the entrance to the ballroom as Robin scoured the room looking for the group. Brian was startled to see Jill, who looked awkward and uncomfortable. He hoped the music would finish and the group would return to the table so he wouldn't have to be alone with Robin and Jill, a prospect he did not relish. *Now that would be a difficult situation,* he acknowledged to himself.

He saw Robin point in his direction, and whisper something in Jill's ear. They both moved toward him. Brian was trapped, but rose to greet them.

"Glad you're feeling better, Jill," he commented.

She ignored him, sat down and looked out at the assembled crowd dancing the night away. Robin stood behind her and glared at Brian looking for a reaction. Brian looked at his son, and wondered whether his son knew about his liaison with Jill earlier that day. Had she told Robin? He sensed it was possible she had.

The eyes of the two men met in an uncomfortable silence as Jill sat between them continuing to gaze out over the dance floor kicking her foot gently, wondering what would happen next as the palpable tension engulfed her.

CHAPTER 15

The tempo of the music changed to a slow fox-trot.

Brian, not wishing to engage in a conversation with his son, turned his attention to Jill.

"Jill, so glad you're obviously feeling better," he repeated. "Please, have the first dance of the evening with me." Brian smiled as he extended his hand for her to join him. She was nervous, and wary of his motives.

Robin purchased a drink at the bar and sat at the table by himself, watching Jill and his father, disgusted and angry with both. *This will be a night for drinking*, he thought, knowing his relationship with both of them would never be the same.

"What kind of a stunt were you pulling by not showing up for dinner this evening?" Brian demanded sternly, but softly, in Jill's ear, his smile now gone. "From now on, you show up for every meal and involve yourself in all the planned party events. I don't care how you feel. Do you get me?"

Jill was silent.

"I said, 'do you get me'?" Brian repeated even more firmly, tightening his grip on her waist. She nodded.

"That's good. You don't want your little game to be over so soon, do you?"

"No," she said quietly.

"Why, Jill. So glad you are obviously feeling better,"

Sylvia exclaimed as she and Richard shuffled past them, giving Brian a dirty glance at the same time.

The music stopped. Jill smiled feebly. "It was just a small headache. Thankfully, it's gone now. I should probably have a dance with Robin. I'm sure you would like to dance with each other," she continued, joining Sylvia and Brian's hands.

Richard excused himself, leaving the anniversary couple alone.

Jill wondered where Robin was, since he was not at the table. Looking around, she saw him getting another drink from the bar. She waited alone at the table for a short while, hoping he would bring her a cocktail. She looked at all the other passengers around her, all laughing and having a good time. How she had messed things up. She felt sorry for herself, and was furious that Robin had hit her, but her real vitriol and hate was toward Brian. She saw Sylvia, and wondered what her reaction would be if she knew of her husband's dalliance earlier that day.

Her mind snapped back to reality as Robin sat down next to her.

"Can we dance?" she asked him, concerned he was drinking heavily.

"Yes, my love. Let's party!" he replied sarcastically. Anyway, he didn't feel like being with Marshall and Alicia, who were headed in their direction. As Robin and Jill left, Marshall excused himself for the restroom, while Alicia tapped her foot, watching the crowd bopping about joyously. She passed the time, observing the ladies and their differing styles and fashions. *I don't care for what Laura's wearing. The outfit's a little too young for her.*

There was a drum roll from the stage. The bandleader seized the microphone, and announced, "Ladies and Gentleman, we will now take a five minute break. Please don't leave — we are just getting warmed up. In the next segment we have some wonderful guests and an evening full of surprises."

Everyone returned to the table. Sylvia looked across the room and saw Denise still seated with the captain. Closer, Richard Manning seemed to be eyeing her group, making her slightly uncomfortable. She smiled at him.

"David, I think it is our turn to spring for a round of drinks," Laura prodded.

"Not for me, thanks," Brian jumped in, covering his half empty glass with his hand. "I'm doing just fine for right now."

"Robin, could you give me a hand please?" David inquired, and the two of them left for the bar.

Stephanie and Jean-Louis came back and seated themselves between Marshall and Marina.

David and Robin returned a few minutes later with the drinks, David placing a large glass of scotch on the rocks in front of Brian.

"David, I told you I don't need another drink," Brian protested.

"Ah, but you want one, Brian. There's a difference. Besides, let's not forget it is a special occasion."

"Well, here's to the happy couple," toasted Laura. "Cheers!"

"Cheers!" everyone echoed in unison half-heartedly. The tone was definitely muted and an uneasy silence fell upon the table.

"All this dancing is quite exhausting!" exclaimed Sylvia, fanning herself. "Will any of you ladies accompany me to the powder room?"

They all departed, with the exception of Jill, who remained quietly with the men. She was not in the mood to be in the company of the women. She really didn't know where she wanted to be. She didn't want to be alone in her cabin, but she was not really in the party spirit.

Within minutes, the ladies returned, as the band struck up and started their next segment. The captain, followed by Denise, led the Conga line which brought everyone out of their seats, except for Stephanie who always considered the conga silly. She remained alone at the table watching the people kicking their legs from one side to another. While she enjoyed her wine, the whole line disappeared onto the terrace before returning the other side of the ballroom a few minutes later. As soon as the song finished, she joined her husband on the dance floor.

The band leader positioned the microphone at the center of the stage.

"Ladies and Gentlemen, before the break, I promised you that we would have some surprises. We are most privileged this evening to have some very distinguished guests," he announced proudly. "Will you please put your hands together for the popular singing sensation, Mister David Clayton?" It was more of a command than a request. The spotlight fell on David and Laura on the dance floor.

"Maybe, you would sing one of your hit songs for us?" the bandleader coaxed, as the crowd applauded enthusiastically.

David headed toward the stage, and after a brief conversation with the band, started to croon one of his well known hits. Having no one to dance with, Laura sat down at the table and watched her husband, wondering if he would ever be able to forgive her. She knew he was being overly civil out of his devotion to Sylvia, but was unsure what would happen when they returned to California. *I can't believe I was so reckless.* Brian was swirling by in front of her, quite the cool one, and poor Sylvia was so oblivious. She watched Brian with disdain.

"Perhaps we should join Laura," Marina suggested to Todd. "It doesn't seem right she should be sitting by herself."

"Would you feel the same if it was Jill?" Todd asked, slightly tired of his wife always wanting to leave the dance floor and bail someone out.

Marina ignored his comment and headed toward Laura.

"Todd, I'd just *love* to boogie with you," Laura gushed as she grabbed Todd's hand before he could sit down, totally ignoring Marina.

Marina was stunned. *I should have known better*, she thought as she watched Laura twirling with her husband.

As she listened to David segue from his first hit song to the last of his hits, she looked at her husband. She loved him so much, and mourned his foundering career. She blamed Brian for that, and there he was, arms around Sylvia, appearing so happy while Marina's own future was so uncertain.

David's solo ended, and it was Todd's turn to receive the accolades and be welcomed onto the stage by the bandleader. David headed back to his seat as did Laura, where they were joined by Sylvia and Brian.

Repaying the courtesy, Marina pre-empted Laura. "David, isn't it about time you asked me for a dance?" She stood up and waited for him to escort her to the floor.

"Laura, we haven't danced this evening," Brian commented, extending his hand. Laura did not wish to dance with him, but protesting would have created an uneasy atmosphere.

It was Sylvia's turn to sit alone, and savor the atmosphere. She watched and listened to Todd singing his solo. She had to agree his voice was not what it once was. He started into a medley of his hit recordings, clearly intended to impress Brian. She felt a degree of nostalgia overcome her, and all the memories evoked by the songs he sang, and which had made him famous. Her mind wandered down memory lane.

Todd finished his turn at the microphone to polite applause and scattered 'bravos' and whistles. The party all returned to the table and their drinks. Sylvia was enjoying herself. The next song was a cha-cha.

"Robin, aren't you going to ask your Mother for a dance?" she quipped.

Sylvia started the cha-cha movements as she headed toward the floor, followed by her son and the other pairs. Brian and Jill were left at the table.

Brian totally ignored her. Uncomfortable, Jill excused herself and left for the powder room. The evening was in full swing. Clearly everyone was having a good time. Brian watched his wife laughing with their son, as they swayed in time to the music. He looked at Stephanie who was now paired with David. Laura looked slightly awkward with Jean-Louis, who was obviously struggling with the rhythm of the Latin American beat. Marshall and Marina seemed to be engaged, as were Todd and Alicia. He was troubled by Alicia though, and wondered why she seemed distant with him of late. *I'll find out from Sylvia what the issue is.*

He eyed Richard Manning across the room, and thought how rude it was to ask Sylvia for a dance since they didn't know each other that well, having only met earlier that day.

He noticed Denise was sitting this dance out and engaging the Captain in repartee. He cast his mind back over the events when they were all young together back in the 1960's, and the paths their lives had taken since.

He finished the drink David brought him and contemplated getting another, but instead, sat back and watched the festivities.

The cha-cha finished and the band switched to a rumba. Everyone continued to sashay with each other, not missing a beat.

A couple of minutes later, Jill returned from the powder room, and saw Brian leaning forward. She sat across from him. He seemed strangely silent.

"Brian, are you all right?" she inquired suspiciously. There was no reply. She moved around the table. *Maybe he's dropped off to sleep*, she thought. She shook him on the shoulder. He didn't move.

"Brian, are you all right?" she repeated, now a little anxious. She nudged him a little firmer.

Brian slumped sideways as his arms sprawled onto

the table knocking over several glasses in the process. He lay motionless.

Jill placed her hands over her mouth and gave a blood curdling scream, as she realized Brian was dead.

CHAPTER 16

From across the room, the captain darted towards the Sinclair table. On his way, he saw Maurizio entering the ballroom.

"Maurizio, fetch Doctor Raymond. Quick!" he commanded. The band stopped playing as confusion and mayhem dominated the dance floor.

Sylvia rushed off the floor, and was the first to arrive at her husband's side.

"Jill! What happened?" she screamed, trying to lift her husband.

Jill stood dumbfounded.

Sylvia turned around to the sea of faces now surrounding her.

"Help! Help! Somebody, fetch a doctor please!" she pleaded.

"He's on his way," the captain reassured her, arriving shortly after her at the table. He moved her gently to one side. "Does your husband have any medical history?" he enquired loosening the tie quickly and opening Brian's shirt buttons. He placed his ear against Brian's heart.

"Only high blood pressure." She was sobbing. "Please! Please! Save my husband." Stephanie pushed through the onlookers and put her arms around her mother to comfort her, as the rest of the Sinclair group gathered around.

The doctor arrived hastily with his medical bag, followed by Maurizio and three cruise staff holding a stretcher.

"Please, everyone! Please stand back," the captain commanded.

The doctor opened the shirt further and positioned his stethoscope over various chest parts, as the captain explained that Brian suffered from high blood pressure.

As the crowds from the dance floor started to get closer, the captain pushed them away demanding more space. He indicated to the band to start playing the music again.

The conductor cued the band.

"Ladies and gentleman, please return to the dance floor and join us for a polka. The night is still young. Let's see everyone on the floor." The band started to play.

After a few attempts at artificial respiration, the doctor realized it was hopeless. He looked at the captain, and shook his head so subtly that no one but the captain knew Brian was dead. Turning to Maurizio and fellow crew members, he gestured for them to move Brian onto the stretcher. The captain took Sylvia's hand.

"Why don't you and just the family members come with me? We'll go to the infirmary."

Sylvia was still bewildered.

"He is going to be all right, isn't he? I mean they can save Brian, can't they?"

"Ssshh, Mother. Let's just go with the captain," Stephanie said soothingly.

The doctor led the way to the infirmary, and Maurizio and the other crew members followed carrying Brian on the stretcher. The captain put his arm around Sylvia and guided her out of the ballroom. Jean-Louis and Stephanie started after them.

"The captain said 'family members', Jean-Louis," snapped Robin, finishing his drink, before leaving the table. "I don't think that includes you."

Stephanie turned on him. "You're drunk! Why don't you just go and throw yourself overboard?"

"You'd like that, wouldn't you? But then you still wouldn't inherit the old man's fortune, if anything happens to him."

Laura moved between them.

"What the hell's the matter with you two? Don't either of you care about your father? And what about what your mother must be feeling?" she charged angrily.

David stepped up.

"Why darling, you're absolutely right. It's wonderful that you have Sylvia's frame of mind so close to your heart."

His sarcasm was lost on the rest of the group.

"Why don't we all go down and wait outside the infirmary, so we can be there and hear the latest on Brian?"

Jill, who had been stunned and in a state of shock since she had watched Brian fall across the table, suddenly regained her composure.

"Don't any of you get it? Brian's dead, I'm telling you," she said haltingly.

"Oh, shut up!" exclaimed Stephanie. "I'm not listening to any more of this. Come on, Jean-Louis." She grabbed his hand and headed out of the ballroom.

"Jill, why would you say such a cruel thing?" asked Marina.

"It's true, I'm telling you! Remember, I was the one who first touched Brian."

"You can say that again! And then some!" Robin interjected caustically, evoking a contemptuous glare from Jill.

Marshall, as was his custom, took charge.

"There is nothing to be gained by all of us standing here by the dance floor, speculating. David is right. Let's go to the infirmary. By now they'll have something to tell us, for sure."

He ushered everyone out of the ballroom.

Denise, still seated at the captain's table, appeared to be mildly curious about what had transpired at the Sinclair table, but stayed exactly where she was.

Richard had also been following the happenings from his table just across the dance floor. After everyone from the Sinclair table had left, he followed them discreetly down the corridor and slipped out the side door onto the deck, where he could observe any comings and goings in the shadows. He lit his pipe, and puffed it slowly, as he heard the sounds of the foghorns above him, and the gentle sounds of the waves against the boat as it steamed steadfastly along its way.

Inside the infirmary, the captain waited with Sylvia until Robin, Stephanie. and Jean-Louis arrived, wondering what had kept them so long.

He then broke the news about Brian. The doctor elaborated, saying he presumed it was as a result of a heart attack.

Sylvia turned to her daughter as they both started to cry in each other's arms. Jean-Louis tenderly touched his wife on her shoulder, annoyed that she had turned to her mother for solace instead of to him. Robin raced outside, pushing his way through the group, and headed toward the deck, where he immediately vomited over the railings. Marshall followed him.

"Robin! What's up?"

"Dad's dead!" he blurted out. He started to sob.

Marshall was not a demonstratively affectionate man. He straightened up.

"Come back inside, Robin. You must be strong for your mother. She needs you now."

"Just go away! Please just go away and leave me alone!" Robin continued between the tears.

Marshall paused. "Do you want me to tell the others?"

"Do what you damn well want. Just please leave me alone."

Relieved to be extricated from the situation, Marshall returned to the infirmary. Richard heard the exchange from his quiet position in the dark corner, and watched Robin stagger slowly along the deck, occasionally grabbing the railing to steady himself. The investigator then turned his attention to the group waiting outside the infirmary.

"It appears Jill was right. Brian is dead," Marshall somberly informed the stunned little gathering.

The captain emerged to an onslaught of questions from the assembled friends.

"I think the best thing you can do, is go back to your cabins," he said firmly but gently. "The doctor is still checking Mr. Sinclair."

"But I need to be with Sylvia. She's my best friend," interjected Marina.

"Please, I must insist that you all vacate this area, and return to your cabins," the captain continued, ushering them along the corridor. He listened to their stunned comments between each other, as they disappeared down the hallway.

Richard stepped out of the shadows.

"Captain, in case you need my assistance, I'm a retired private eye," he said, offering his business card.

The captain took it, but appeared confused. "Why would I need your help?"

"Oh, with regard the demise of Mr. Brian Sinclair."

"Surely, you don't suspect foul play?"

"Why, Captain. Things are never quite what they appear. Perhaps, we can have a chat tomorrow morning?"

"Mr. — er — Manning," the captain stumbled, trying to read the name on the business card in the dimly lit hallway. "I think this is premature. The doctor still needs to complete his examination."

"As you wish, Captain. But should you need my expertise, please feel free to contact me. You have access to my cabin number."

He turned and headed off down the deck, leaving behind a very troubled and perplexed captain.

CHAPTER 17

Early the next morning, the captain was already in his office seated behind the large mahogany desk. The desk was orderly, as would befit a disciplined man, and there were several, neatly arranged photographs on the sides. The walls were adorned with an assortment of pictures of his ship, various awards and certificates of accomplishment. The furniture in his office was masculine, with the upholstery of the chairs and couches reflecting a naval motif with anchors, buoys, and seagulls. The sun was pouring through his window, creating a bright and airy atmosphere.

"Do come in," he called out loud in response to the knock on the door. Richard entered. The captain rose to greet him.

"Oh, good of you to come so promptly, Mr. Manning. I hope you didn't mind me calling you." The two men shook hands. "Can I pour you some coffee?"

"Thank you. I take it black, the way God intended, and no sugar. I'm pleased you called, and as I said last night, I'll be happy to assist in any way I can. I was just surprised you called so soon. Do you have some information?"

The captain gestured his guest to take a seat on the couch while he poured the coffee.

"Well, actually, I was interested in what prompted you to think Mr. Sinclair might have been murdered. By the way, please help yourself to the Danish." He pointed to the plate of assorted pastries on the coffee table between them.

Richard shrugged. "Oh, I don't know. Nothing concrete. More instinct and intuition, I suppose. Call it a hunch that comes after a lifetime of investigative work. As an observer of human nature, I was fascinated by all the comings and goings at the Sinclair dance table last evening. I noticed the body language and facial expressions of the various members of the party as they interacted with each other both on and off the dance floor. Also, there was the occasional turn when I was on the dance floor I overheard some comments giving me cause to think all was not well. But surely, you must have contacted me today for more than the opinion I expressed to you last night. "

"Well, Doctor Raymond called me this morning. He did not give me any specifics, other than he is not convinced Brian Sinclair died of natural causes. He is still checking, and will have his full report to me later today."

"Interesting. Did he tell you what symptoms led him to believe the death may not have been a natural one?"

Before he could answer, there was another knock at the door. The captain rose to answer it.

"Why, Mrs. Sinclair, please come in."

Sylvia was looking very pale and drawn. As she removed her dark glasses, the captain observed the red around her eyes, revealing how much she had been crying.

"I am so sorry to come unannounced. I was going to make an appointment, but there was no one at your assistant's desk."

"No, I have him doing some errands for me right now."

The captain did not disclose he was checking Richard Manning's credentials, before imparting too much information. "Please join us for some coffee and Danish pastries. I don't know if you've met Richard Manning."

"I had the pleasure of playing bridge with Mrs. Sinclair yesterday afternoon." Richard turned to Sylvia. "Please accept my most sincere condolences, Mrs. Sinclair."

"Thank you, Mr. Manning," she replied.

"Maybe I should return later, Captain?"

Before the captain could answer, Sylvia interjected. "That won't be necessary, Mr. Manning. After all, I have intruded on your meeting with the captain."

The captain brought the coffee tray to the table, and proceeded to pour Sylvia a cup. Her hands shook as she took a sip.

"Captain, I would like to thank you for your kindness and understanding last night. Unfortunately, I am going to need your help with making some arrangements when the ship docks at New York."

"Mrs. Sinclair, you are not to worry about a thing," the captain reassured her. "My staff will make all the necessary arrangements for your husband's body to be flown back to California on the same flight as yourselves. I will personally oversee everything. If there is anything I can do for you any time — day or night — I am at your disposal."

"You're too kind." Sylvia appeared very stoic as she dabbed her eyes with the lace embroidered handkerchief she was clutching in her hands. It was clear she was maintaining a brave front, and appreciated the captain's genuine concern.

"Mrs. Sinclair, please forgive the indelicacy of the question, but is there any reason you can think of why anyone would want to kill your husband?"

"Mr. Manning!" the captain interjected forcibly.

"That's quite all right, Captain," Sylvia said slowly, but calmly. She turned to Richard and gave him an icy stare.

"Just what are you driving at, Mr. Manning?"

Confronting grieving family members was a part of his job Richard hated. He always felt uncomfortable. But, he knew if a murder was actually committed, he had but a few days before the ship arrived in New York's harbor in which to solve the mystery. Once the ship docked and everyone went their separate ways, the case would be turned over to the proper authorities and it would be impossible.

"I am merely wondering if there was anyone you know, who would like to see Mr. Sinclair out of the way, or who would benefit from his death."

"Mr. Manning, I think the doctor concluded last night my husband died of natural causes." Sylvia was terse and stern.

"Actually, Doctor Raymond has suggested your husband may not have died from natural causes. I am awaiting his final report. I know how hard this is for you, but anything you can think of that may help ..." The captain stopped.

Sylvia's eyes welled up with tears, and once more she wiped them with the handkerchief. The two men sat quietly, waiting for her to compose herself. Looking downward, she shook her head. Suddenly, she thought back to London, when she heard the conversation between David and Laura in the bedroom. She remembered David screaming to Laura that he wanted to kill Brian. Yet she refused to believe he was capable of murder.

Richard recognized the knowing look that appeared on Sylvia's face.

"What is it, Mrs. Sinclair? You've remembered something?" he coaxed.

"Oh no, it's nothing," she said dismissively.

"Please. Let us determine that," the captain offered gently, reaching out and sympathetically touching her hand.

Sylvia trusted the captain. He really was being very kind to her. After a few moments pause, she recounted how she had overheard David saying how he wanted to kill Brian.

"But why would David Clayton want to kill your husband? What possible motive could he have? Wasn't your husband his manager and agent?" Richard asked.

Sylvia turned and looked at Richard directly. "My husband had slept with his wife that afternoon, Mr. Manning. She was supposed to be with David in the recording studio that day."

There was an awkward silence.

Sylvia rose from her chair. "Now, if you gentlemen will excuse me, I think I have had quite enough for one morning. In fact, much more than I think I can handle during the last twenty four hours. The kind doctor gave me some kind of sedative, as I am sure you can imagine I did not sleep too well last night."

The gentlemen rose from their seats.

"Allow me to escort you back to your cabin, Mrs Sinclair," the captain offered.

"That's quite all right, Captain." Sylvia headed toward the door. As she turned the handle to leave, she stopped as if in thought. Then she turned to look at them both. "Since you are both investigating this, you may wish to investigate what Denise Parker's motives for being on this ship are."

"Denise Parker? What does she have to do with this?" the captain asked.

"That's what I would like to know," Sylvia retorted. "Didn't you know at one time she was engaged to my husband? We hadn't seen her for years and then she shows up on this cruise ship at the very same time my husband and I are celebrating our silver wedding anniversary. More than a little odd, wouldn't you say?" She left the two men and closed the door behind her.

"Well, we have barely started, and we have three suspects already," declared Richard. "Shall we commence by paying a little visit to David Clayton first?" He headed toward the door.

"Three? How do you arrive at three suspects?"

"David Clayton, Denise Parker and Sylvia Sinclair."

"Surely you can't think Mrs. Sinclair killed her own husband? You saw how shocked she looked at the suggestion her husband may have been murdered."

"Ah, you have been far too long at sea, Captain. Surely you know hell hath no fury like a woman scorned? Just as Mr. Clayton was furious his wife slept with Brian Sinclair, Mrs. Sinclair had to have been equally as devastated at her husband's infidelity — especially on the occasion of her silver wedding anniversary. She may have just appeared shocked we were on the murder trail so quickly."

As they left the captain's office, the captain's assistant was back at his desk.

"Excuse me, Sir. Here is the information you were seeking." He handed the captain a sheet of paper.

It was the report and validation the captain had been seeking on Richard Manning. He was both relieved and elated the private eye was held in such high regard by the British authorities and Interpol.

On the way to the Claytons' cabin, they passed Doctor Raymond's office.

"Would you mind if we stop in?" Richard enquired of the captain.

"I told you, Doctor Raymond would let me have the final report when he was ready. I am sure he will not have it yet."

"Oh, I do not wish to see the good doctor or his report at this time. Actually, I would like to see the log of who actually visited his office since the ship set sail."

The captain obliged and the doctor fetched the patients log for them to review.

"Captain, are you familiar with the cabins reserved by the Sinclair party?"

"I can check for you if you like," he said dialing the phone number of the appropriate office. He scribbled the names and numbers of cabins reserved for the Sinclair party, and the occupants' names. Since he knew all the suites were in one group, he was surprised the Sinclairs only occupied one of the two Grand Suites. He asked who was occupying the suite across from them.

"Here is the list of the cabins and occupants you requested. I have one more piece of interesting information for you. The Grand Suite across from Mr. and Mrs. Sinclair is occupied by Denise Parker."

Richard raised his eyebrows with genuine surprise. He looked at the names on the list the captain had given him, and perused the doctor's patient log.

"How will the doctor's patient log help?"

"There are two possibilities. At this point in time, I have to assume it was either poison or conflicting medication that caused Brian Sinclair's death. Either the murder was pre-meditated, which means the killer could have brought the necessary supply on board with him or her from England or America, or something occurred since the ship departed that precipitated the reason for the murder. If this was the case, the only access one could have to any poison or medication would be through this office."

"But, that would be impossible. Doctor Raymond would know. He is here at all times, as is his nursing assistant."

"Of course. But if the doctor is called from his office to take a phone call in the reception area, the patient would have access to the medicine chest."

"That would have to be split second timing."

"That's all it normally takes," Richard concluded. "Well, well, well, now. Look at this log. We have some very surprising and interesting names on it."

He passed the log to the captain, who was taken aback when he saw the list.

"Looks like we have our work cut out for us, Mr. Manning," he exclaimed.

"Indeed we do, Captain. Indeed we do. And by the way, please call me Richard."

The captain nodded, as the two set off to David and Laura's cabin.

CHAPTER 18

The captain knocked on the door of the Claytons' cabin.

"Why, Captain, do come in." David welcomed his visitors inside, looking slightly askance at the unknown gentleman standing alongside.

"I hope we're not intruding. I don't believe you have met fellow passenger, Richard Manning," responded the captain as he entered.

Richard and David shook hands and David gestured for them to be seated.

"No intrusion, none at all. In fact, Laura and I were about to come and visit you. We've tried calling Sylvia Sinclair all morning, and have knocked on her cabin door several times. There's been no response. We're more than a little concerned."

"Don't worry, Mr. Clayton." The captain allayed David's fears. "Mrs. Sinclair has already stopped by to see me this morning. Given the circumstances, she's holding up extraordinarily well. Maybe she decided to take a bit of fresh air on deck before returning to her cabin. It's also possible she just wants to be alone."

"Well, that's a relief. Must say, it was a bad break for her. Poor Sylvia! Who would have thought Brian would go just like that?" David gestured by snapping his fingers in the air. "It was a terrible shock to us all."

The captain looked at Richard, as if beseeching him to take the lead. Richard picked up on the cue.

"Well, we're not certain he did go 'just like that'," Richard remarked, watching David's face for any reaction. He was distracted as Laura emerged from the bedroom. The gentlemen all rose.

"Darling, you know the captain, and this is — er — Richard Manning," said David.

"How do you do, Mr. Manning?" Laura extended her hand. "Please, do sit down." She sat on the sofa next to David and turned to the captain. "To what do we owe the honor of a personal visit, Captain?"

"Darling, it appears Brian may not have died from natural causes, as we thought last night." David held his wife's hand.

"Yes, Doctor Raymond thinks there may have been some 'foul play'," Richard continued, still looking for a reaction.

Laura was aghast. "Well, that's preposterous!" she exclaimed. "Who in the world would want to kill Brian?"

There was a pause. No one wanted to speak.

"The Captain and I had hoped you may be able to enlighten us on that score," Richard finally commented, breaking the silence.

"Richard Manning is a private investigator," noted the captain, realizing he had failed to explain why Richard was with him.

"Well, surely you don't suspect either of us?" David said with a degree of indignation. "Brian and Sylvia have been close friends of ours for years. Brian has been my manager for I don't know how long. They are like family, aren't they, darling?" he said, seeking confirmation from Laura.

The captain and Richard exchanged glances.

"Do you deny ever threatening to kill Mr. Sinclair?" Richard was confrontational.

"Captain. Mr. Manning. You will leave our cabin right now." David demanded as he rose and strode toward the door.

Richard was unfazed. "Apparently, you were overheard threatening to kill Mr. Sinclair during your stay at the Dorchester Hotel in London."

David stopped dead in his tracks and swirled around. Laura sat upright on the sofa, looking at David, and wondering how he would handle the situation. They had both forgotten David's outrage of that day.

"I understand Mrs. Sinclair returned from her shopping early while you were in London. From her room next door, she overheard much of your conversation — and your threat," Richard continued.

Laura was shocked and embarrassed. She stood up and moved toward the window by the deck and looked out. She realized how bad it looked for them.

David hedged. "Sylvia must have misheard." He was buying time.

"I don't think so," Richard said slowly. "She heard enough to know there had been some, shall we say, 'infidelity', that afternoon. You certainly had a motive."

"Sylvia can't possibly think I had anything to do with Brian's death. It's insane," David replied.

Laura, realizing the consequences of her actions in London, immediately saw an opportunity to save both her husband and her marriage. She was fuming that Sylvia had divulged personal details to a total stranger knowing if the story leaked to the press it would have a damaging affect on her husband's career and image. She moved toward David's side, and linked her hand through his arm.

"Mr. Manning, my husband is totally incapable of murder. I should know. His words were just expressions of anger at that moment. If Sylvia was aware of what happened at the Dorchester Hotel, she would have plenty of reason to kill her husband. After all, hell hath no fury like a woman scorned."

"Funny you should mention that phrase, Mrs. Clayton. It was the exact phrase I used a short while ago. And speaking of a woman scorned, just what was the depth of the relationship between you and Mr. Sinclair?"

David stepped forward. He was angry. "I don't think that is any of your damn business. Captain, I must ask you and Mr. Manning to please leave our cabin. I will not listen to any more of these false slurs and innuendos."

"It's all right, David." Laura was happy to answer the question, if for no other reason to assure her husband it was nothing more than a fling. "Mr. Manning, Brian and I had a brief tryst that one afternoon," she lied. "Nothing more. I must suggest you speak to Mrs. Sinclair. She *clearly* had the motive," she said emphatically.

"Ah, but Mrs. Sinclair did not have the opportunity. At this time, we have to assume Mr. Sinclair was poisoned — presumably at the table near the dance floor. Mrs. Sinclair was never alone at the table," Richard countered.

"But she could have poisoned him at the dinner table.

Who knows what pills were in that Harrods pill box she passed to Brian every night just before coffee."

"What pills?" Richard asked quizzically.

"Oh, blood pressure pills. Brian had been taking them for years. Sylvia had purchased this beautiful little pill box from Harrods while she was in London. She passed it along to Brian every mealtime."

"Besides," said David, putting his arm around his wife. "You may also wish to speak with Brian's son, Robin, who had more of a reason than Sylvia to kill Brian. It was only yesterday afternoon he was threatening to kill his father."

"Oh, really?" Richard appeared nonchalant, but now his curiosity was piqued. "What possible reason would he have for killing his father?"

"I suggest you ask him before coming in here with your wild accusations. Now I really would like you both to leave," David said sternly, happy the suspicions were deflected away from himself.

Richard and the captain rose and headed toward the door.

"Oh, just one question before I leave," Richard pondered. "Mrs. Clayton, I notice yesterday afternoon, you visited Doctor Raymond's office. What ..."

Before he could go any further, Laura interrupted him. "There's not a crime in that, is there? While I was by the pool, I developed a terrible headache. David came to the cabin and got me an aspirin, but it didn't help. I visited the doctor to see if he could give me anything else. I wasn't there more than five minutes. Doctor Raymond seemed pre-occupied. He was back and forth, and in and out of his office."

"Thank you, Mrs. Clayton. I thank you both for your time."

David suddenly appeared sheepish and contrite. He steered them toward the door.

"Look, gentlemen. You know, this could harm my career, my reputation. I hope I can count on your discretion to keep this to yourselves."

The captain spoke for the first time. "Mr. Clayton, there will be no mention of this to anyone, provided everything you have told us is true. Good day to you both."

"What in the world were you thinking throwing Sylvia under the bus like that?" demanded David as soon he closed the door.

"I can't believe Sylvia would accuse you of murdering Brian," Laura lashed back. "And the words you used at the time are pretty damning. I had to shift the focus to someone else."

"And why didn't you tell me you went to the doctor yesterday afternoon? When did you go?"

"I didn't think it was that big a deal. The aspirin you got me didn't work. When we came back from the pool and you went for a shower, I just popped along to see the doctor. What's more mystifying is why you didn't tell me about Robin. Why didn't you tell me he had threatened to kill Brian — and why? If I'd have known that, we would not have had to point the finger at Sylvia."

"Laura, it is almost as if you believe them. Do you really think I killed Brian?" He looked at her incredulously.

She stared back. "You haven't answered my question about why Robin wanted to kill his dad."

Outside in the corridor, the captain and Richard made the short walk to Denise Parker's cabin.

"Well, it appears you now have four suspects, Richard," noted the captain.

"Five," Richard corrected. "There's David Clayton, Sylvia Sinclair, Denise Parker, Robin Sinclair and Laura Clayton." He knocked on the door of Denise Parker's Grand Suite.

"Laura Clayton? Why would you think Laura Clayton is a suspect?"

"She lied to me about the afternoon tryst at the Dorchester. I could tell. That was not the only time she and Brian had been together. Maybe he broke the relationship off. My dear Captain, maybe Laura Clayton is the woman scorned."

CHAPTER 19

"Enter!" shouted Denise. She was lying comfortably on the chaise longue in her suite, a sleep mask covering her eyes, and the back of her hand over her forehead as if suppressing the pain from a hangover.

The captain coughed. Denise bolted upright, and removed the mask from her eyes.

"My apologies, Captain. I was expecting my bloody mary from room service."

She stood up to greet her guests, straightening her caftan dress and fluffing her hair. She immediately shifted into her onstage personality.

"Miss Parker, may we trouble you for a few moments?"

"Why Captain, you can trouble me all you want, as long as you call me Denise," she teased, suddenly adopting a provocative stance. "And who is this handsome gentleman?" She extended her hand with her palm down, for Richard to kiss it.

The captain was clearly embarrassed. "This is Richard Manning, he's a private investigator."

"Pleased to meet you, I'm sure, Mr. James Bond," she joked as she giggled.

Richard took her hand and shook it. "I've always been a big fan of yours Miss Parker."

"That would be Denise, Mr. Bond," she smiled. "Please, both sit down. And just what are you investigating?"

"Miss Parker — er — Denise," the captain corrected

himself. "You may not have heard the very sad news." He paused. "Last night, Brian Sinclair died."

Denise's face turned ashen. She reached for her cigarette case, and lit one up, inhaling furiously, her hand trembling nervously. She looked downward. The memories of her youth and the years she and Brian were together came flooding back.

"There is a distinct possibility he may have been murdered."

Denise stiffened. *Where's that drink I ordered*, she thought. She desperately needed it now.

"It appears you knew Brian Sinclair," the captain continued.

"We go back many years, Captain. What of it?" Her voice was clipped.

"Is it true that at one time you were engaged to be married to Mr. Sinclair?"

"That was a *very* long time ago," she responded firmly. "In case it has escaped your notice, Brian and Sylvia Sinclair are celebrating their silver wedding anniversary on this cruise," she said acidly.

Richard was intrigued as he noticed her face showed no emotion. She revealed no more than a blank stare.

"May we ask how you came to be on this particular cruise? The very cruise the Sinclairs were having their celebration," he asked.

She looked him directly in the face. "It's very simple, Mr. Manning. My agent booked me on this cruise. That's what agents do."

"What is your relationship with Brian and Sylvia Sinclair now?"

"What kind of a question is that? I don't have a relationship with the Sinclairs. I haven't seen either of them for years."

"Yet, you were praising Mr. Sinclair at your concert the other evening, and you were talking with him alone at the table during the dance last night."

"Mr. Manning, were you spying on me? Surely talking with someone doesn't constitute a relationship?"

"What were you talking about?"

She could see the probing, and where it was headed. "I do not care for the tone or tenor of your inquiry, Mr. Manning." She turned to the captain. "Do I really need to answer all these questions?"

"We'd appreciate your cooperation Miss — er — Denise. I know it's difficult."

"No, Captain, and no, Mr. Manning, I did not murder Brian Sinclair if that is what all this is about. If I were to kill anyone, it would be that bitch of a wife of his." She stumped out her cigarette firmly in the ash tray.

There was a knock at the door. This time, Denise rose to answer it. A steward entered with a tray bearing a bloody mary and placed it on the coffee table.

"Will that be all, Ma'am?"

"Yes, thank you." She tipped him and closed the door behind him.

"I would have asked you both to stay for a drink, but I think our conversation is just about completed here, is it not?" she said rhetorically, and with no degree of tact. "I'm sure you both have better ways to spend your time today." She picked up her drink and stirred it with the celery stick, before taking a large gulp.

"Before we leave, maybe you could tell us of anyone who might wish to see Mr. Sinclair out of the way, as it were?" Richard asked.

Denise continued to toy with her celery stick and the drink. "Mr. Manning, in this industry one has many enemies — especially someone with the power and stature of Brian Sinclair."

"But, who aboard this ship?"

Denise shrugged and thought for a moment. "You may wish to have a little chat with Alicia Hardcastle. She is not the cool, calm, classy lady you might think. If anyone had reason to bump off Brian, it would be her."

"And what might that reason be?" Richard asked.

"She had an affair with Brian Sinclair's former business partner, who happened to be my best friend. There was some shady business about her former 'boyfriend's' death." She was not going to elaborate.

"Information about which she just found out through you, no doubt," Richard observed.

"You catch on real quick, Mr. Manning. Alicia came to my dressing room after the concert. You're damn right I told Alicia what she needed to know. And, while you're at it, after you have interrogated her the way you have interrogated me, you might want to also have a chat with Marshall Thornton."

The captain tried to be tactful. "We hope you don't think of it as an interrogation, Denise. We're just trying explore all the options and motives. You've been most helpful to us."

"Anyway," Denise continued. "He's been Brian

Sinclair's right hand man for years and years. He's the suave and debonair bachelor who is never far from Brian and Sylvia. Wonder why he has never married?"

Both gentlemen were nonplussed at the rhetorical question.

"He is still in love with Sylvia Sinclair after all these years. The poor sap. He came to see me yesterday morning. There's nothing he wouldn't do for that broad. If Sylvia had any reason to get rid of Brian, she would only have to say it to Marshall and he'd do it. You can take that to the bank." She paused to light up another cigarette. "And you know what the irony of it is? Both Sylvia and Brian are clueless. I'll bet Brian had no idea that all these years his partner's been in love with his wife."

"Are you saying Marshall and Sylvia are lovers?" Richard asked.

"Good God, no! Sylvia is way too stuffy and too much of a prude to go for any extra-marital excitement in her life. Not sure her husband exercised the same judgment, though," she offered gratuitously. "No, Marshall is just one of those long-suffering fools that loves from afar and who loves to wallow in his own self-inflicted misery." She shook her head sideways, as she pondered Marshall's life incredulously. "One thing, though. If you came here looking for the murderer and someone with a motive, you're barking up the wrong tree. Now, gentlemen, if you'll both excuse me. You know where the door is. I think you can let yourselves out."

She extinguished her cigarette, placed the sleep-mask over her eyes, laid back down on the chaise-longue and rested her head on the cushion.

"Thank you for your time, Miss Parker," said the captain.

"Denise," she groaned.

"Thank you, Denise," he corrected himself yet again. The two men left her suite.

"Why don't we go back to my office, and see if there is any report from Doctor Raymond?"

"Good idea."

They walked out onto the deck and strode toward the captain's office. The sun was shining brightly as the awnings flapped in the soft, gentle breeze. The sound of laughter wafted from the swimming pool as the children splashed away. They passed a group of people playing an enthusiastic game of deck quoits. But none of these shipboard attractions caught their attention, so pre-occupied were they with their mystery.

"Well, the plot certainly thickens," observed the captain. "Guess we can now add a couple more suspects to the list. But I think it is safe to say we can remove Denise Parker from the list."

"Why do you say that, my dear man? Have you forgotten a woman scorned?"

"For heaven's sake, Richard. That was over a quarter of a century ago. If she had any intent on revenge, she would surely have done something years ago?"

"Don't be too sure. Sometimes revenge doesn't go away. Sometimes it eats away. Besides she was not honest with me, when she said her agent booked her on the cruise. Of course, the statement was essentially true, but there was more than that. I can always tell when someone lies. No, dear Captain, we cannot eliminate Denise Parker from the suspect list, any more than we can eliminate either of the Claytons or Mrs. Sinclair. We still have to talk to Robin Sinclair — and now it appears we need to talk with Alicia Hardcastle and Marshall Thornton. We have a busy day ahead of us. I played bridge yesterday afternoon with Mrs. Sinclair, Mrs. Hardcastle and Mr. Thornton. There were definitely some interesting, shall we say, 'dynamics' among those three."

CHAPTER 20

"Instead of going to my office, let's stop off at Doctor Raymond's. It's closer," suggested the captain.

The two of them walked along the corridor leading to the medical quarters.

"Sorry Captain, I've not had time to complete my examination yet — certainly not to my satisfaction. We've had an unusually high number of patients this morning. There seem to be more passengers suffering from sea-sickness than usual. Not sure why. This has been a very smooth crossing so far."

"No problem," said the captain, concealing his disappointment. "I'll check back in a couple of hours." He turned to Richard. "Where do we head to next?"

"Maybe, we should see if we can find Robin Sinclair, since he apparently made a direct threat on his father."

They headed toward Robin's cabin, and knocked on the door. Footsteps were heard inside. The captain knocked again. There was the sound of shuffling toward the door.

"Who is it?" mumbled a voice from inside.

"This is the Captain."

"Yeah? What the hell do you want?" Robin barked.

"We need to talk to you."

"Who the hell is 'we'?"

Robin's voice was slurred. The captain spoke softly to

Richard. "I think he's drunk. We'll probably not get much from him." Richard nodded in agreement.

"Mr. Sinclair, please let us in," the captain said more forcibly.

He heard the sound of the door being unlocked from the inside. Robin was still wearing his dressing-gown. His face was unshaven, his hair disheveled. The redness around his eyes was an indication of just how much he had been crying. He was holding a cigarette in one hand, and an almost completely consumed bottle of scotch whiskey in the other."

"May we come in?" the captain asked.

"Suit yourself," Robin responded dismissively.

Both men stepped inside, Richard closing the door behind them.

"I would like to introduce you to Richard Manning."

Richard extended his hand. "I'm sorry about your loss, Mr. Sinclair."

Robin ignored the offer to shake hands and took a swig from his bottle of whiskey. He wiped his mouth on the dressing gown sleeve. "Yeah? Well, who the hell are you anyway?"

"I'm a private investigator." He thought the shock treatment would work better with Robin than the more gentle approach, and continued, "I'm here with the captain to investigate the possibility of your father's murder."

Robin glared at him, then looked at the captain. "What's he doing here? I thought you said my father died from natural causes?"

The captain replied. "That's what we presumed last night. Doctor Raymond now has some evidence indicating that may not be the case. We are awaiting his full report."

Robin banged the bottle of whiskey down on the table and let it go. He flopped down on the sofa and stretched his crossed legs onto the coffee table. "Then what the hell are you both doing here? Why aren't you out there finding which son of a bitch did it?"

"You don't seem overly surprised at the possibility of your father's death not being a natural one." Richard sat down in a chair across from him.

"Hell, no! I'm not surprised at all." Robin turned and flicked his cigarette out the porthole window, and promptly reached for another one. He paused for a moment. "I wouldn't put it past my scheming sister and that bastard frog of a husband of hers. They knew the old man was going to cut them out his will. Dad hated that son of a bitch!"

Richard remembered seeing Stephanie leave her father on the dance floor having engaged in some kind of verbal altercation. He had assumed she was Robin Sinclair's sister, given her resemblance to Sylvia. "Why were they being cut out of your father's estate?" he asked.

"Oh, God," Robin moaned, running his fingers through his hair, and rolling his head backwards. "Do we really have to go through all this now?" he pleaded.

Richard ignored his question. "It appears you also had a reason for killing your father."

"What?" Robin was aghast. "Be careful where you go with those accusations, mister. You'd better be prepared to back that statement up." He pulled his legs off the coffee table and sat upright.

Richard remained calm. He'd dealt with volatile

situations on numerous occasions. "Apparently, you threatened to kill your father in front of David Clayton yesterday afternoon."

Robin cast his mind back to the previous day, and recalled his conversation. He was furious with David for betraying his trust, and wondered how much of their verbal exchange David had revealed. He hoped David hadn't told him about his father's tryst with Jill. "And did he tell you why?" Robin asked gingerly, fearing the worst.

"No, he didn't. I assume you will tell me why."

"Well you assume wrong, mister." Aware that Richard Manning did not know the reason for his threat gave him confidence. He was in a confrontational mood. "What I said yesterday afternoon was in the heat of the moment. People make dumb statements like that all the time." He stood up.

Richard rose and faced him. "Really, Mr. Sinclair? Maybe we should be the judge of what was said 'in the heat of the moment,' and whether it was cause enough for murder."

Robin was now really angry. "You are not going to judge a damn thing. Now, just get the hell out of my cabin."

The situation was getting out of control. The captain rose from his seat, and using his hands, placed a safe distance between them.

"Mr. Sinclair, please understand that Mr. Manning is just trying to get to the bottom of your father's death. He must follow every lead. I know this is a rough time for you. Please bear with us."

Robin glared at the two of them, before sitting back down. He picked up the bottle of whiskey, and emptied it down his throat. He lit his third cigarette.

"You'll both leave my cabin this instant. I have nothing more to say to either of you. If you are going to formally charge me with murder, then go ahead and do it. If not, I have nothing more to say unless I have an attorney present."

Realizing any attempt at getting any further information from Robin was futile, they left.

"Interesting that Robin mentioned he would not talk to us again unless he had an attorney present," Richard commented as they walked along the corridor.

"Why's that?" asked the captain.

"People don't normally mention having an attorney present unless they have something they're hiding. We'll need to go back to the Claytons, if necessary, and obtain more details. Obviously David Clayton was not telling us all he knew."

Robin heard their muffled voices further down the corridor. They were knocking on the door of someone else's cabin. He heard them go inside. While still wearing his dressing gown, he slipped out of his cabin and ran along the corridor to Jill's cabin. With his key, he let himself in.

Jill was lying on her bed, feeling sorry for herself. She let out a mild scream of surprise, until she realized who it was. She jumped up.

"Oh Robin, I'm so very sorry." She ran to put her arms around him.

He pushed her down on the couch.

"Don't you even touch me, you tramp!" he thundered. "They're now saying that Dad's death may have been murder. You better not have had anything to do with it."

Jill started to cry. "What are you talking about? Who would murder your father? Why would I murder your father? You're not making any sense. Robin, I swear, I don't know what you're talking about."

"Good. Then when they come to talk to you, you'd better not mention anything about your disgusting little fling with my father yesterday afternoon. Do you get it?" He pointed his finger in her face. He was as angry as he was the day before.

"Who? Who is coming to talk to me? I don't understand."

"The Captain and some private eye. Just keep your mouth shut. You hear me?"

Jill nodded, as she tried to wipe the tears from her eyes. He was so menacing and threatening, she was now afraid of him.

Robin turned and left her cabin. He heard the Captain and Richard's voices emanating from Alicia's cabin, and hastened to the door to listen. But before he could hear anything, he heard the sound of footsteps coming up the staircase. Hastily, he bolted back inside his cabin, wondering what had prompted the captain and private investigator to question Alicia. Why weren't they questioning Stephanie and Jean-Louis as he suggested? Although as long as they didn't think it was him anymore, that's all that mattered.

CHAPTER 21

Alicia was surprised to see the captain and Richard Manning when she answered the knock on her cabin door.

"Mr. Manning, surely it is too early in the day for a game of bridge?" she inquired feebly.

"May we come in?" the captain asked. "Actually, we have come to discuss Brian Sinclair's death, Mrs. Hardcastle."

"Oh?" Alicia sounded surprised as she opened her cabin door further, and gestured for them to sit on the couch. Both men sat down, and looked at her wondering where to start.

"We're sorry for the loss of your friend, Mrs. Hardcastle. I understand you have been a friend of the Sinclairs for a long time now," the captain started.

"Yes. It's quite tragic, isn't it?" Alicia responded. "I'm still in a state of shock. I suppose we all are. My heart goes out to Sylvia."

Richard sensed she was a little nervous. He decided to get straight to the point. "There's a possibility that Brian Sinclair's death wasn't accidental."

Alicia was astonished. "What? You mean to suggest he was murdered?" she asked incredulously. "Who would do such a thing?" She looked back and forth at both men for a response.

For part of the previous afternoon, Richard had

partnered Alicia while playing bridge and had observed her quiet outward calm, and cool exterior. He was struck by the totally emotionless face when she opened her dealt cards, and the manner in which she bid her hand. Her demeanor was most perfunctory. He knew he would have to catch her off guard, to get anything from her.

"Denise Parker thought you may be able to shed some light," he suggested.

Alicia shot him a swift, disapproving glance that certainly expressed her displeasure. He had elicited the reaction he was seeking.

"What has Denise to do with this?" she inquired, deeply suspicious of how much the singer had shared about their conversation and their history.

"It seems you and her best friend had some kind of a relationship."

Alicia looked downward uncomfortably as she considered that the secret she had held for all these years might have been exposed. Her hand fidgeted on the arm of her chair. She turned to the captain.

"Do I really need to be subjected to this line of questioning?"

"It would be helpful to us, Mrs. Hardcastle," he said as if to encourage her.

"Why is it necessary to have Mr. Manning here?"

"I've asked him to help with my inquiry given his knowledge and expertise as a private investigator. You can be assured of his complete discretion."

Alicia paused. Then, in a clipped tone, said "If you are referring to my affair with Greg Calderman — that was a long time ago. What of it?"

"It would seem that, until recently, you were under the impression he committed suicide," Richard prodded.

Alicia sensed the direction of Richard's statement and side-stepped. "As I said, that was some twenty-five years ago. Since then, I met and married a man who made me very happy. We had a wonderful marriage until he died a few months ago."

"Did your husband know of your previous affair?"

"Mr. Manning, many people have relationships before they marry. Do you know of your wife's former relationships? Or for that matter, was your wife the one and only relationship you have had?" she countered, turning the tables on the questioner. Richard considered her suggestion an affront.

"Mrs. Hardcastle, I doubt if my personal life would be of much interest to you. However, your affair with the former business partner of the very man who invited you to be one of his select few guests at his silver wedding anniversary party is of significant interest to me. Especially since the host of this party is now dead, and who, it appears, may have had a hand in the very death of the man you once loved." Richard was forceful.

"The man with whom I had an affair," Alicia retorted.

"The man you loved," Richard responded more forcibly and loudly.

The captain intervened. "Richard, I am not sure it is necessary to be quite so harsh."

"I am merely trying to get at the truth, which I don't think I am getting from Mrs. Hardcastle." He stared straight into Alicia's eyes, as she looked back defiantly.

There was an uncomfortable pause. Alicia realized

Denise Parker had probably relayed everything, and that it was pointless trying to conceal anything from the two prying gentlemen in her cabin.

"All right," she said testily. "Yes, I did love Greg, and yes, I was pregnant with his child when he committed suicide — or at least, I thought he committed suicide. It was certainly what we were all led to believe, anyway. Our relationship would not have gone anywhere. He was married, and would never have divorced his wife. I didn't care. I loved him and I was happy. When he died, I was frightened, scared and alone. I was very young at the time. The pain lasted for years." She stopped and was pensive, as if reliving the past memories. "I was stunned when I saw Denise Parker two nights ago. The visions of the past came flooding back. I knew he was her best friend. I went to her dressing room to talk with her."

"Is that when you learned your lover did not commit suicide? From Denise Parker?" Richard intervened.

Alicia nodded.

"How did you feel when you learned that Brian Sinclair may have had a hand in the death of your lover?"

Alicia was exasperated. "Mr. Manning, he was a *former* lover, and he had a name. His name was Greg Calderman." As if to drive home her point, she repeated, "Greg Calderman. Do you get it?"

"My apologies," Richard offered with sincerity.

Alicia could tell from the look on his face he meant it. She thought for a minute while regaining her composure.

"When Denise told me he was murdered, and that Brian and Marshall may have played a part, I was in total disbelief. I never really thought Greg was capable of suicide, but I guess I was just too young and naive at the time to consider murder. I needed an abortion that I had to confront. I was all alone at the time. Besides, what could I have done, anyway? Called the police?"

"You could have spoken to Brian Sinclair." Richard suggested. "Obviously you wouldn't have suspected him at the time."

"I didn't know Brian and Sylvia then. It was coincidence that I met Brian later playing tennis at the country club. My husband Bruce and I began playing bridge with the Sinclairs. We became good friends."

"Did you ever tell them of your affair with Mr. Calderman?"

"Of course not. Apart from Denise Parker, I'm not sure anyone else knew. But then, since Denise shot her mouth off to you, who in the world knows who else she has told."

"Do you think she ever told Mr. Calderman's wife?" the captain asked.

"Terri? I wouldn't imagine so. Denise doesn't have much class, but even she would not want to hurt Terri. Besides, she told me she hadn't seen Terri since the day of Greg's funeral."

Richard was concerned they were straying too far from his probe. "Once you got over the shock of being told that Brian Sinclair or Marshall Thornton probably murdered Mr. Calderman, how did you feel then?"

Alicia knew precisely where the line of questioning was leading.

"I'm not too sure that I am over the shock, as you put it, of the possibility of Brian or Marshall murdering Greg.

It has been very uncomfortable for me being in Brian's presence, and certainly being at the bridge table with Marshall yesterday afternoon. Between receiving the news from Denise two nights ago, Brian dying in front of us all last night, and now you tell me that Brian, too, may have been murdered. I'm sure you will both agree that I have had a lot to contend with since I have been aboard this ship. I have suffered no end of migraine headaches these last couple of days."

"Is that why you went to see Dr. Raymond yesterday morning?"

Alicia bristled. "I thought conversations and visits between a patient and a doctor, are supposed to be sacrosanct and private?"

"They are." Richard acknowledged. "But, the logging of your name in the register at his office isn't."

"I went to see the doctor to get some sleeping tablets, if you must know. I had not slept the previous night after my conversation with Denise Parker. Surely you can understand that?" she said acidly.

"I can indeed, Mrs. Hardcastle. I can indeed." Richard turned to the captain. "I don't believe we need to trouble Mrs. Hardcastle any further."

Alicia was relieved, and made her way toward the door to show her guests out.

"You have been most helpful, Mrs. Hardcastle. Maybe we can play bridge again before the ship docks?"

Alicia looked at him warily. "Maybe," she replied, as she shut the door behind both men.

"Another woman scorned?" asked the Captain.

"You're a quick learner, Captain. But Mrs. Hardcastle

was quite forthcoming. Either because she was unaware of how much Denise had told us and did not want to get caught in a lie, or maybe she thought that if she came clean, it would absolve her of any suspicion."

"And did it?"

"No. It is too early to rule out any of the suspects at this time. And we still need to see the Sinclair's daughter and son-in-law as well as Jill Potts."

"What about Todd Hammond and his wife? They are also friends and guests of the Sinclairs. Are they suspects?"

"Maybe. We will visit them last. See if they have anything to offer. But, at this time, it doesn't appear as if they have any motive."

"What about Marshall Thornton? Is it possible he could be involved? You haven't mentioned him."

"That's because we are heading to visit him right now, my dear fellow."

CHAPTER 22

"I was just heading out for a stroll. It seems such a beautiful day outside," Marshall commented to the captain and Richard as they entered his cabin. "I do hope this won't take long."

"As long as necessary," Richard responded, as he seated himself in an armchair. Marshall seemed mystified. He looked at Richard and then at the captain.

"We won't take up too much of your time, Mr. Thornton," assured the captain.

"Oh, please. Call me Marshall."

The captain nodded. "How long had you known Brian Sinclair?"

Marshall shrugged. "Oh, we knew each other for years. I was the lawyer for Sinclair Records. We first met back in our college days. He was my closest friend. I was best man at Brian and Sylvia's wedding." The captain and Richard exchanged glances, not unnoticed by their host. "Why do you ask?" he continued.

Richard was direct. "Were you also the Sinclairs' personal attorney?"

"Of course. I handled all of their legal affairs."

"Then, presumably you would be in a position to know who the beneficiaries are in Brian Sinclair's Estate?"

Marshall was offended. "Mr. Manning, I am not sure I appreciate the impertinence of your question. How dare you …." He was cut off by the captain.

"My apologies, Marshall. I haven't explained the purpose for our being here."

"Then perhaps it's time you did, Captain." Marshall was clearly irritated.

"There is a strong possibility that Brian Sinclair was murdered. I have asked Richard Manning to assist with an inquiry, given his experience as an investigator."

Marshall was stunned. He rose from his seat and turned toward the porthole, looking away from his two visitors. He placed his hands in his pockets.

"That's ridiculous!" he finally exclaimed. "Why in the world would anyone want to kill Brian?" He turned and looked at both men.

"As it happens, we have already established quite a list, Mr. Thornton. Now, could you please answer my question?" Richard persisted.

"Of course I know who the beneficiaries are." Marshall was still agitated. "They will be named at the reading of the will, which will be on our return to Los Angeles. To divulge any information prematurely, would be a breach of attorney-client privilege."

"But Mr. Sinclair was more than a client. He was your best friend. Maybe, you could share the beneficiary list with us now. It would certainly help with our investigation. Surely, you would want to assist us in any way we can to establish the possible murderer of your best friend?"

Marshall thought for a minute. There were advantages to revealing what he knew. He would be able to see where the gentlemen were headed in their investigation, and deflect any possible suspicion they may have toward him.

"Of course, the information will be kept totally confidential," the captain reassured him.

"Brian had two wills drafted. We spoke just before we left for the cruise. He said both wills were in his fireproof safe at his home in Beverly Hills. He had signed and dated one, and had it notarized. Naturally, I had signed both."

"Why would he have two wills?" the Captain inquired.

"He was always at odds with his daughter and threatening to cut her out of his estate. One will was drafted with Stephanie as beneficiary and one without. I have no idea which is signed."

Richard was curious. "Who stood to benefit if Mr. Sinclair's daughter was removed from the will?"

"Stephanie's share was distributed among the remaining beneficiaries."

"Equally?" Richard continued.

"Not exactly."

"Oh? Who was the beneficiary who stood to gain the most?"

Marshall was quiet. He looked at Richard.

"Actually, I was." He saw the looks on their faces, and knew precisely what both were thinking. "Brian wanted to make sure both his son and wife had substantial shares in Sinclair records, but wanted neither to have dominant control of the company," he added hastily. "But, if Stephanie remained in the will, Sylvia had control of the company."

Richard rose from his chair, and placed his hands behind his back. "Which does give you a motive, Mr. Thornton, does it not?"

"I'd be very careful with your allegations, Mr. Manning," Marshall threatened. "I'd be very careful, unless you want to be sued for slander."

"Calm down, Mr. Thornton. I was merely making an observation, not an accusation. You stated earlier no one had reason to kill Mr. Sinclair. You just provided a reason why you might want to."

The captain noticed that Marshall was now becoming angry, and intervened. "Marshall, are you sure you cannot think of anyone who would want to kill Brian Sinclair? Anyone at all?"

Marshall thought again. "Well, I suppose, if I think about it, one could almost come up with a reason for everyone," he said dismissively. "I guess Stephanie could have a reason, if she was aware she was being eliminated from the will, but I don't know if she knew."

"She did, Mr. Thornton. She did know. I overheard her on the dance floor with her father, when she was discussing it," Richard recalled.

"Then maybe you should be talking to her, instead of to me," Marshall fumed.

Richard ignored his comment. "I'd also like to know of the relationship between yourself and Mrs. Sinclair."

"Sylvia Sinclair is a classy lady. There *is* no 'relationship' between Sylvia and me. She is a great and dear friend, and the wife of my best friend." Marshall was indignant.

"It has been suggested that you are in love with Mrs. Sinclair. Is that true?"

"You've been speaking to that Denise Parker, haven't you?" Marshall fired back.

"It has also been suggested to us that there was something more sinister about the death of Greg Calderman than was reported at the time."

Marshall's face reddened. "Get out of this cabin! Get out of here immediately, before I slap you with one hell of a lawsuit, Mister," he thundered.

Richard stood and observed the expression on Marshall's face.

"Captain, please remove this gentleman from my cabin." Marshall commanded.

"We're sorry to have distressed you," the captain said adopting an apologetic tone. He put his hand behind Richard's back and guided him to the door of the cabin.

"Actually, I'd like you to stay for a few moments, Captain. I would just like Mr. Manning removed."

"Good day, Mr. Marshall. Thank you for your help." Richard nodded to the captain and left.

Marshall realized both his visitors had already obtained a lot of information before arriving at his cabin. He was not sure of exactly how much, but it did not look good for him. Since the finger of suspicion was now pointing at him, his mind raced feverishly as to whom else could have a possible motive for killing Brian. He took a sanctimonious stance with the captain.

"Captain, I am truly offended by the suggestions made here about my character."

"Once again, I apologize. I hope you understand our desire to just get to the truth."

"Your apology is accepted, Captain. Now that I have thought about it, I can think of a couple of people who stand to benefit more than I from the death of Brian."

The Captain was intrigued, as Marshall explained further.

"First, there is Jill Potts. I know Brian checked her background a while back. Apparently Sylvia neither liked nor trusted her. Brian always relied on Sylvia's instincts. He confided in me that he had quite a dossier on Jill's background. He didn't elaborate of course, but I know he indicated she has a past. Then there is Todd Hammond who is on the verge of financial ruin. He has a new contract which I have signed, but it still requires Brian's signature. It will be the salvation for Todd and Marina." As if reading the Captain's mind, Marshall continued. "If there are contracts pending at the time of Brian's death, all contracts become effective without his signature."

"That's a rather unusual procedure, isn't it?"

"Yes, it is. But that is how Brian always wanted it. It had been a long standing procedure. Should anything happen to either of us, he did not want his contracts voided due to lack of a signature. Especially in his case, since it may be a while before a new CEO is appointed. Amazing, he had such foresight," he added drily.

"Makes sense I suppose. Was Todd aware of his contractual status?"

"Of course he was. He was constantly on the telephone asking about it, and when would Brian sign it. He was becoming quite a pest."

"How about Mrs. Hammond? Was she aware?" The captain was pleased with what he picked up from Richard about questioning, and knew Richard would be impressed with his revelations.

"She must have been. One must assume Todd told her. Now Captain, I really don't believe I can be of any more assistance," hoping he had planted the seeds of doubt about himself.

"Absolutely. You have been most helpful. Thank you so much for your valuable time and insight. Rest assured, it will all be kept confidential. And don't bother, I can see myself out." He left.

As soon as the captain stepped outside, he almost bumped into Richard, who was standing right outside the door.

"Oh, Richard. Do I have some information for you," he enthused.

"Quite," Richard responded. "Mr. Thornton just provided the motive for Todd and Marina Hammond." The captain was aghast.

"Mr. Thornton's voice travels. I could hear everything he said from out here in the corridor. I guess we will be paying the Hammonds a visit after all," Richard concluded.

CHAPTER 23

"Well, good morning, Captain," greeted Marina breezily. "To what do we owe the pleasure of this visit?" She gestured with her hand to welcome them in. Todd stood up and extended his hand to the Captain.

"May I introduce Richard Manning," the captain announced.

"My wife was a great admirer of yours, Mr. Hammond. She had all your records." Richard commented as he and Todd shook hands.

"*Was* an admirer?" grinned Todd. "Is she no longer a fan?"

"My wife is deceased, Mr. Hammond."

Todd immediately felt uncomfortable.

The captain deftly switched the subject. "Richard Manning is a private investigator."

"Sounds positively ominous, Captain. And how intriguing. By all means, please sit down." Marina seemed quite mystified.

"How long had you both known Brian Sinclair?" The captain looked at both for a reply.

Marina was astounded at the question. "Sylvia is my best friend. We have been friends since childhood. I was bridesmaid at their wedding," she confided.

"And Brian was best man at our own wedding," added Todd. "We all go back a long way together."

"Have you continued to be close friends all this time?" Richard asked.

"What kind of a question is that?" Marina chortled at the absurdity. "Of course we have been close friends all this time. Sylvia and I talk and meet constantly for lunch. As for Brian and Todd, well, their business activities and schedules preclude us from socializing as often as we would like. But we are here with them for their silver wedding anniversary, so I am sure they consider us among their 'inner circle'. Naturally, we are both devastated by Brian's death, aren't we Todd?" She looked to her husband for reassurance. "I spoke to Sylvia this morning, but she said she wanted to be alone. Why all these silly questions anyway?"

"It seems that Brian Sinclair's death may not have been the result of natural causes," said the captain.

"Good Heavens! Whatever leads you to believe such a thing?" Marina sounded genuinely surprised.

"The ship's doctor seems to think that foul play may have been involved. He will have his final analysis for us later," Richard elaborated.

"Nonsense!" exclaimed Todd. "That's the most ridiculous suggestion I've ever heard. I can't think of anyone who would want to get rid of Brian. Everyone liked him," he declared somewhat unconvincingly.

"Not according to Denise Parker," Richard shot back. "She said that everyone in the recording business has enemies. I believe she said especially someone of Mr. Sinclair's stature."

"I hope you're not building a case for Brian's death

based on the notions of that woman, are you?" Todd's tone conveyed the contempt he felt for Denise.

"I take it you don't care for Miss Parker?" Richard asked.

"Not in the least, Mr. Manning. But then I stand corrected, now you have mentioned her name. I suppose if anyone had a reason for killing Brian, it would be Denise. After all, Brian did dump Denise for Sylvia."

Richard studied Todd and noticed how much age and the reported bouts with alcohol had taken its toll. How different he looked from all the photographs on the album covers his wife had in her collection. He decided to throw them off guard. "Yes, and we are given to understand quite a few others have a motive for seeing Brian Sinclair dead. Indeed, it appears you were having some contractual difficulties with Sinclair Records."

"Just what are you driving at, Mr. Manning?" Marina was suspicious and her voice, terse. Her face turned slightly pale, as she linked her hand through her husband's arm, as if to assure him of her support.

It's almost as if she's protecting him, Richard thought. "I'm merely stating I am under the impression that since Brian Sinclair will obviously not be returning to his business, your husband's contract will be renewed for another ten years. Had he have been alive, it is possible that he would not have renewed the contract. Isn't that correct, Mr. Hammond?" he said forcefully.

Todd wondered who would have divulged such information. Marshall was the obvious suspect. But then it was plausible that Robin would have known, and quite conceivable that Brian would have mentioned it to Sylvia, he thought. "Just who have you been talking to Mr. Manning?" he asked.

"Who I have been speaking to is irrelevant, Mr. Hammond. The point is I am correct in my understanding, am I not?"

Marina intervened. "And what if you are? Surely you are not suggesting that would be a reason for my husband to kill the person who was best man at his wedding?"

"Maybe. Maybe not," Richard replied. "But, I must confess Mrs. Hammond, I overheard you last night, while dancing with Brian Sinclair, pleading your husband's case and for renewal of the contract. The conversation did not sound overly friendly to me. In fact, it sounded quite confrontational."

"Now look here!" Todd Hammond interjected.

"It's all right, Todd." Marina stopped her husband. She faced Richard Manning and added, "Yes, it is true I discussed Todd's contract with Brian. Why wouldn't I? I love my husband deeply. And yes, I was angry with Brian. He was treating Todd despicably. Todd made a lot of money for Sinclair Records over the years and Brian was casting him aside like a used tissue. I would do anything for my husband and his career, but that does not include murdering the husband of my best friend. Besides, there are a number of record companies that would be more than happy to have my husband recording for them." She was stern and forceful.

As Richard had heard Todd Hammond's singing the previous evening he was dubious about the claim, but it was evident to him Marina clearly would do anything for her husband. "Ah, but are there, Mrs. Hammond? Forgive me for saying this, but, even I am aware it has been quite a while since your husband has had a hit record. I am not sure of the value or content of your contract, but would a contract with another recording company offer you the same financial lifestyle?"

Marina was beginning to wonder whether Sylvia had betrayed her. She recalled the dinner conversation she had had at the Beverly Hills Hotel before the cruise, when she had confided the financial difficulties she and Todd were encountering.

"And what do you know of our finances, Mr. Manning?" Todd demanded to know. He ignored the comment about the lack of a hit record. "Just who have you been talking to? Whoever it is, is woefully misinformed."

"I wouldn't be too sure of that, Mr. Hammond." Richard eyed both Marina and Todd, aware that neither was being particularly forthcoming or candid. He sensed that Brian and Todd had not been as close as Marina indicated. Nor did he believe it would be as easy for Todd Hammond to obtain a contract with another recording company so easily. He suspected from this couple there was genuine despair at the prospect that Todd's contract would not be renewed with Sinclair Records.

"Apart from Denise Parker, do either of you have any thoughts on anyone else who may have cause to want Brian Sinclair dead?" the captain asked aloud, again defusing what he saw as a tense situation developing.

"I'm confident your doctor will soon ascertain he was

mistaken, and will find there was no foul play whatsoever," Marina asserted. She rose to signify the meeting was at its end.

"Gentlemen, I would have to agree with my wife." Todd rose and stood next to Marina. "Despite my earlier comments about Miss Parker, I believe Marina is right. Your doctor is simply mistaken."

Both Richard and the captain were certain they would not obtain any more useful information from this couple and made their exit.

Outside the cabin, the captain immediately dismissed the Hammonds as viable suspects.

"On the contrary," Richard argued. "It is very plausible Todd Hammond could have murdered Brian Sinclair. I saw no remorse from him about the loss of the person who was best man at his wedding. I could also see where he would want to maintain his lifestyle, if not for himself, at least for his wife. It is equally possible his wife may have committed the crime. She clearly loves her husband, and as she herself stated, would do anything for him. She said that does not include murder. I absolutely differ with her. I believe Mrs. Hammond would do anything protect her husband. We must also remember she was Mrs. Sinclair's childhood friend as opposed to Mr. Sinclair's."

"I suppose so," the Captain agreed as he pondered Richard's observations and reason.

They headed along the short corridor toward Jill's cabin on the other side of the stairway.

Almost as if it was an afterthought, Richard continued, "Of course, I wouldn't rule out the possibility of both of them being involved. Both Hammonds had a singular goal.

Both had the same motive and the same opportunity. It is a distinct possibility they could have acted in collusion. Did you notice neither of them referred to Mr. Sinclair as their friend? Mr. Hammond referred to the deceased as the 'best man at his wedding', as did Mrs. Hammond. She also referred to him as 'the husband of her best friend' but neither of them said he was their friend. Most peculiar, don't you agree?"

The captain weighed the possibility for the first time of the Hammonds being partners in crime, as they knocked on the door of Jill's cabin.

CHAPTER 24

J ill was still on her bed in a pink nightgown when there was a knock on the door. She quickly wrapped a robe around her and opened the cabin door with great trepidation. She was apprehensive upon seeing the captain and instantly recognized the man accompanying him as the one who was dancing with Sylvia while she was dancing with Brian the night before. These had to be the gentlemen Robin had told her about. *Well, at least it's a relief it's not Robin.*

The captain introduced himself and Richard Manning.

"May we come in for a few moments, Miss Potts?" the captain asked.

Jill nodded, as she opened the door and motioned them to sit down. Nervously, she sat down opposite them. Richard noticed how frightened she seemed.

"Robin told me you may be paying me a visit," she informed them timidly.

"Oh, he's been to see you?" Richard was surprised. "What did he have to say?"

Jill shrugged and looked vacant. "Not much of anything really," she replied vaguely. "He just mentioned you would be asking me some questions about the death of his dad."

"Did he mention why we would be asking you about the death of Brian Sinclair?"

"He said his father may have been murdered." Jill was cautious and wary.

"Can you think of any reason why anyone may want to kill his father?"

Jill shook her head.

"Yet you were the one who found Mr. Sinclair," Richard persisted. "You were at the table with him."

"But I wasn't at the table the entire evening. I don't know what happened. Honestly, I don't." She was scared and defensive. "I wasn't feeling well all evening. I didn't even go for dinner."

"You were also one of the last to speak to Mr. Sinclair. After all, you were dancing with him minutes before you found him dead."

Jill cast her mind back to the night before, and how Brian had threatened her, and yet now he was the one who was deceased. She was lost in her thoughts as she relived the evening in her mind.

"Miss Potts?" Richard engaged her again.

"I'm sorry. What were you saying?" Jill snapped back to reality.

"Did Mr. Sinclair say anything to you while you were dancing? Did he express any fear for his life?"

Jill shook her head again.

"You and he were alone at the table when you discovered he was dead?'

"Yes. David — that's David Hammond — had bought a round of drinks for us all. Then, everyone went for a dance, leaving Brian and me at the table alone. I went to the restroom, and when I returned I discovered him just lying there. I touched him, and that's when he rolled over." A sudden look of realization appeared on her face. "Say, David brought the drinks. I watched him hand the Scotch directly to Brian. Do you think he could have slipped something in the glass? Brian had said he didn't want another drink, but David insisted." She was excited at her revelation.

Richard smiled feebly. "How was your relationship with Mr. Sinclair?"

"Oh, Robin is my boyfriend."

"No, Mr. Sinclair, the senior." Richard was exasperated.

"What do you mean? What kind of relationship?" Jill twisted uneasily in her chair.

"Don't play games with me, Miss Potts. You know very well what I mean. Did you have any kind of relationship with Brian Sinclair?"

Jill cast her eyes downward as she fiddled with the chord on her robe. After a brief pause, she looked back at Richard Manning. She didn't know what to say.

For both men, her non-response told the story. Recalling what Marshall had said about Brian Sinclair's background check on the lady now before him, Richard continued aggressively. "Miss Potts, were you either threatening or blackmailing Brian Sinclair?"

Jill was getting more frightened. "No! I never threatened or blackmailed Brian," she responded defensively. She turned to the captain as if for support. "What reason would I have?"

Richard didn't believe Jill Potts was as naïve and as innocent as she was professing. "Miss Potts. I would advise you to be very truthful when answering these questions.

You have every good reason to extort from Brian Sinclair." Even though he had no concrete evidence, he thought he would call her bluff. "I understand Mr. Sinclair had quite a rap sheet on you."

Jill panicked, like a deer caught in the headlights. *How much he did he know about her past? How did he know anything at all? Who did Brian tell? How many people knew?*

"May I also remind you, Miss Potts, that with all my contacts, all I have to do is to call the authorities, and I will have your entire history within minutes?"

Jill breathed more heavily, feeling trapped. She thought of Robin's warnings and threats to her earlier that day, but was past caring. *To hell with Robin and this entire damn family.* She rose from her seat. "All right, Mr. whatever-your-name-is."

"Manning. Richard Manning," he interjected.

"All right, Mr. Manning. Yes, I may have a past. But, you've got it all wrong. Brian was the one who was threatening me, not the other way around. He was here yesterday afternoon and threatened me."

Richard glared at her. "And just why would he do that?"

"If you must know, we had a fling." She thought back to the first time she saw Brian Sinclair at his Beverly Hills mansion. She was forlorn as she recalled her hopes and dreams and how all her plans had gone awry. "I was dating Robin. But from the moment I saw Brian, I knew I had to have him. I saw his beautiful home. I felt I belonged there. I had grandiose ideas and big dreams of moving in. Sylvia is sweet, I suppose. But, really quite dreary, you know. Brian was a man who lived on the edge. He loved excitement. I could feel it. I could give him that. He had to have been bored stiff with straight-laced Sylvia. On this cruise, with my own cabin, I knew I could seduce him. I was surprised at how easy it was. It was like giving a bottle of Scotch to an alcoholic." She sat down. The two men waited for more.

"Please continue, Miss Potts." Richard's voice softened a bit.

"He came here yesterday afternoon. Sylvia was playing bridge. We had a good time. At least, I thought we did. I know he enjoyed the sex. When I suggested we meet the same time today, he laughed. He said that I was just a bit of fun for one afternoon. It was humiliating. When I told him I would tell Sylvia, that's when he threatened me."

"Is that when he revealed to you what he knew about your past?"

"Yes," Jill nodded.

"What did Robin say when he found out?" Richard was following his hunches. He had observed both Jill and Robin at the table the previous night, and how cold and aloof they seemed to be with each other.

Jill's mood changed. She was now furious. She figured Robin was the one who had told them about her sexual escapade with Brian. How dare Robin come to her and demand she be quiet, when he blabbed everything. She could kill him for making her a suspect, and possibly the prime one at that.

"What did Robin say?" she repeated back. "He was furious with me — still is, but even more so with his dad. If you really want to know, he threatened to kill his dad."

Two can play at this game she thought, determined to get her revenge.

Richard doubted her last comment.

"You would agree though, Miss Potts, you certainly did have a motive for murder, didn't you?"

"Maybe I had the motive, but I didn't commit the crime."

"Really, Miss Potts? I wonder what my check on your background will reveal?" Richard was playing his hunches again.

"I can save you the trouble, Mr. Manning. If you really must know, I shot my step-father." She knew she was cornered and thought honesty might be the best policy.

"So you certainly have the capacity to kill," Richard deadpanned.

Jill glared at Richard contemptuously. She looked him straight in the eye. "My step-father raped me, Mr. Manning. Do you get it? He raped me."

The captain was uncomfortable at the turn of events. "I'm very sorry, Miss Potts." He rose from his seat and turned to Richard. "I don't believe we need to trouble Miss Potts any further, do we?"

As if to make amends, Richard rose and as he headed toward the door, he was reassuring. "Miss Potts, if what you have told us is the truth, I can tell you that all the information will be kept confidential."

Jill was astounded. "And for that I am supposed to be grateful?"

"Good day, Miss Potts."

"Yet, another woman scorned, Captain," he said once

they were in the corridor. "Now let's see what daughter and son-in-law have to say for themselves."

"Do you really believe Jill Potts could have done it?"

"It is certainly possible. She had the motive, the opportunity, and by her own admission she has the ability."

The captain was not convinced. *When a lady has been raped by her step-father, it is a different story,* he thought. He concluded that could be considered justifiable homicide, but decided it best to defer to Richard's superior knowledge.

CHAPTER 25

Jean-Louis only partially opened the door when the captain and Richard knocked.

"Unfortunately, my wife is too distressed to see you right now, Captain."

"My apologies. I know the timing is inopportune. May I extend my sympathy on your loss?"

"What is the meaning of the word 'inopportune'? I don't understand the word." Jean-Louis was constantly troubled by his lack of command of the English language, and his frustration was always reflected in the testiness of his voice.

"I meant, I appreciate this is not a good time to visit, but, if we could have just a few minutes."

"Captain, I told you my wife is not ready for company yet."

Richard intervened. "It is imperative we speak to both you and your wife."

Jean-Louis turned his gaze to Richard, while guarding the entrance to his cabin.

"This is Richard Manning. He is a private investigator." The captain hoped that would be enough for Jean-Louis to bend.

"Yes, we met last night. He was dancing with my mother-in-law. She introduced us."

Stephanie appeared in the doorway, behind Jean-Louis.

"It's all right, sweetheart. They can come in. Captain, I don't believe you have met my husband, Jean-Louis."

Both Richard and the captain extended their hands. "Sincere condolences from us both," offered the captain. "Have you met Richard Manning?"

"Yes." She turned and looked at Richard, while directing her comments at both men. "As Jean-Louis said, he was dancing with my mother last evening, when we happened to dance by. She stopped and introduced us. She didn't explain how or where you met, though."

"We met playing bridge yesterday afternoon. She was my partner, since your father chose not to play."

"She also didn't tell us you were a private detective, Mr. Manning. Why are you here now? Is it just to offer your sympathy or do you have an ulterior motive?"

As they sat down, Richard took stock of Jean-Louis and Stephanie's appearance. She was looking very pale. She had obviously been crying and a crumpled tissue could be seen out the corner of her clenched left hand. Jean-Louis sat next to her and put his arms around her shoulder protectively. His face seemed devoid of any emotion. Certainly he did not appear to be in a state of mourning.

The captain tried to be gentle. "We no longer believe, that is, Doctor Raymond and I, no longer believe that your father died naturally. We have enlisted the very able services and expertise of Richard Manning to assist us in our investigation."

"What? That's preposterous," Stephanie declared in disbelief. The expression on the face of Jean-Louis remained unchanged and dispassionate.

"You don't seem very surprised, Sir." Richard addressed his observation to Jean-Louis.

"I'm not. Not everyone was a fan of the great Brian Sinclair."

"Oh darling, please let's not get into that now," Stephanie pleaded. She reached for his other hand and held it.

"I take it you certainly weren't," Richard encouraged, hoping for more details.

"No, I wasn't Mr. Manning. The relationship, such as it was, between my father-in-law and I was one of mutual distrust and disdain."

"Honey, why are you going into that now?"Stephanie was perplexed.

"It is not a secret. If they don't hear it from me, they will hear it from someone else. They probably already have. Am I correct?"

Both the captain and Richard remained silent.

"You see, Stephanie. Someone has already told them." Returning to face his guests, he continued. "But because I detested the man, it is not enough of a reason for me to kill him. If I were going to do that, I would have done it a long time ago."

"Would you care to elaborate on who else did not like Mr. Sinclair?"

"Excuse me?"

Stephanie translated. "They want to know who else didn't like Daddy." She wiped her nose with her handkerchief.

"Mr. Manning, I am not sure how many people you have spoken to before you came here, but I would almost guarantee everyone you have already seen probably had a motive for murdering Brian."

Richard noted his assessment was a surprisingly astute one. "I am sure then you will appreciate and understand the need to question everyone."

"Stephanie and I have nothing to hide and nothing to fear."

Richard was amazed at Jean-Louis's ability to hold an entire conversation without changing the expression on his face. *What an outstanding poker player Jean-Louis would make*, he mused.

"Well, since you mention it, if it is not too painful for you, Stephanie, maybe you can explain the altercation between yourself and your father on the dance floor last night."

"He means argument, honey." She patted her husband's hand then gave a hefty sigh. "My father and I were never close. We always had a love-hate relationship. We hadn't spoken for a couple of years. Were it not for Mother, we wouldn't be here now. He was always threatening to cut me out of his will, which I never gave a damn about anyway. I thought he would be pleased I'm pregnant and giving him his first grandchild. He was so egotistical he wanted his first grandchild to be Robin's so the baby would have the name Sinclair."

"He even offered to pay for an abortion," intervened Jean-Louis.

Richard raised his eyes as he and the captain exchanged glances. The exchange did not go unnoticed by Stephanie.

"I know what you are thinking Mr. Manning, but let

me assure you, neither of us would kill my father. Jean-Louis had nothing to gain. Since I have already been cut out of the will, I certainly didn't."

"Do you know for a fact you have been excluded from the will?"

Stephanie shrugged. "Well, I just presumed so. Dad was always threatening to. I assume he acted on it. In any event, I would never, ever, hurt Mother. She is too precious to me and I know how much she loved my father. Actually, I need to pop along and see how she is doing any time now, so if you will excuse us." She wiped her nose again with her handkerchief.

"Have you seen or spoken to your mother since last night?"

"Yes, as a matter of fact, I was with her early this morning, just before she left to see you, Captain." She nodded in his direction. "I offered to go with her. She said she preferred to go alone and then she wanted to be by herself for a while. I said I would go along later this morning. Mother has always dealt with her emotions privately. She is a very strong and controlled person."

"Before you leave, can you think of anyone aboard this ship who might wish to see your father out of the way?" Richard probed.

Stephanie was pensive for a moment. "No, I can't really say that there is. They have all been friends of the family for so long." She thought longer, and then added, "Of course, I suppose it could always be Robin's girlfriend. She's most peculiar. But then, all of his floozies are. I don't know what her motive would be though. Then there's that Denise Parker. I'm not sure what's going on there. All I know is that when she walked out on stage the other night, she certainly planted the cat among the pigeons, that's for sure. Everyone's mood seemed to change, especially when she started flirting with Dad. I even commented to Jean-Louis about it, didn't I?" She turned to her husband.

"That's right. I didn't detect anything, but my wife certainly did."

"Did anyone say anything? Any passing comment at all?" Richard asked.

"No, it was like a wall of secrecy came down among the crowd. Clearly there was some ghost from the past, but no one was talking. Everyone was tightlipped. I decided to mind my own business. Sometimes, ignorance really is bliss, Mr. Manning. Now, I really must go and see Mother."

"Just one thing before you leave. I noticed in the visitor's log, that you were both at the doctor's office yesterday afternoon."

"Yes, we were." Jean-Louis was irritated at the intrusion of privacy. "After lunch, when you were playing bridge with Sylvia, we went shopping. My wife became dizzy and giddy. As you now know, she is pregnant. As a precaution, we stopped by to see the doctor. Surely you don't begrudge her that?"

"Ah, yes, of course." Richard commented as he and the captain rose from their chairs and prepared to leave. "It appears that not only did you browse through the shops, but you actually made a purchase at Harrods," he said, noticing a small, Harrods plastic bag with its familiar green and gold logo on the table.

Stephanie stood up, and strode to the door, clearly

agitated. "Mr. Manning, I'm not sure what you are driving at. I don't know what our shopping has to do with anything. If you came here to accuse either my husband or me of killing my father, you're on the wrong track. We've been more than honest with you. The simple truth is you are barking up the wrong tree. We did not do it. Now, I really want to freshen up, and pay a visit to my mother, who could probably use some comforting." She opened the door.

"Once again, I offer my condolences on your loss," the captain stated awkwardly. He wondered exactly how much of a loss Brian Sinclair was to either of them. *Possibly another woman mistreated*, he thought, as he shook Stephanie's hand. It was a thought he knew was on Richard's mind.

"Thank you again for your time," Richard commented as both men exited into the hallway. *These two individuals clearly had plenty of motives between them.* Like the Hammonds, he wondered whether they could have acted individually, or whether they too, could have been partners in crime.

Once Stephanie heard the footsteps fade away, she turned on Jean-Louis. "Why in the world did you mention to them about the abortion? That was like pointing the finger of suspicion directly at us." She threw her hands in the air in exasperation.

Jean-Louis shrugged. "It just seemed the right thing to say and do. I thought if we were honest with them, they will look elsewhere. Maybe they will look for someone who is not telling them the truth. It is those who create a web of lies who are normally the culprits.

Stephanie was not convinced. "There's a difference between lying and sometimes just keeping quiet. I just hope your theory works."

He hugged her tightly, as she nestled her head in his chest and started to cry, as if, for the first time, she was recognizing the impact of her father's death. He kissed her gently on the top of her head.

Now on the deck and out of earshot of the passengers in the cabins they had just visited, there was a sense of urgency in Richard.

"Captain, it is imperative that we have Doctor Raymond's report. It is now critical."

The captain was perplexed. "Why? What have you discovered? I mean why is it critical now?"

"I'll tell you later. In the meantime, if you could get his report, I have a couple of things I need to check out. Maybe, I can meet you in your office in about fifteen minutes."

"All right, I'll see what Dr. Raymond has for us. I need to attend to a few things myself. Let's make it half an hour. You're not thinking that Stephanie is really capable of murdering her father, are you?"

"Well, Stephanie is right about one thing. We *have* been barking up the wrong tree."

With that, he disappeared down the stairs back to the suspect's cabins.

CHAPTER 26

Richard immediately regretted not having waited a few minutes outside of Sylvia Sinclair's cabin. The moment he knocked, he heard Marshall Thornton's loud voice emanating from inside the suite. Had he waited, he may have overheard some illuminating information. As it was, the voice was muffled immediately, and he heard Sylvia's footsteps coming toward the door.

"Why, Richard Manning, I certainly didn't expect to see you again so soon. I didn't think you would have found the culprit yet." Her tone was caustic.

"May I come in for a few minutes? I promise I won't take up too much of your time."

Sylvia thought for a moment, before opening the door wider and allowing him to enter. "You know Marshall Thornton, of course."

Marshall was clearly uncomfortable, but ignored the intruder. "Maybe I should leave now, Sylvia, and come back later."

"It is not necessary, Mr. Thornton. I won't be long." Richard turned to Sylvia.

"Mrs Sinclair, may I see the pill box that you purchased at Harrods?"

Sylvia was astounded and stared at him incredulously. "What?"

"I understand at every meal time you provided you husband with a blood pressure pill that you kept in a pillbox in your handbag. I was told you purchased the little box at Harrods. I would like to see it if I may."

Marshall rose in anger. "Now look here …" he started.

"It's quite all right, Marshall. Please calm down." Sylvia eyed Richard Manning warily and with deep suspicion, but went into the bedroom to retrieve her purse from the previous evening. She placed the box on Marshall's open hand. "Actually, it wasn't every meal time, only at dinner times."

Richard noted the unique motif of the pill box. "Do you mind if I borrow it for a short while?"

"I can't possibly think that it could be of any use to you. Surely you are not suggesting that I placed a poisonous pill in it are you?"

Marshall rose from his seat, clearly agitated. "Really, Mr. Manning! I think your wild theories and innuendos are getting way too much. Mrs. Sinclair is in a state of grief. I must ask you to leave." He stood behind Sylvia and placed his hands on her shoulders protectively.

Richard ignored him. "I understand your husband sat at the opposite end of the dinner table. Whose hands did the pill box pass through in order to get to your husband last night?"

"It so happens, Mr. Manning, the waiter, Maurizio, took the pill box to my husband, on his tray. The pill box only touched my hands and those of my husband."

"Is there anyone else who touched your handbag that evening? "

"Actually, everyone did," she responded. As if to clarify, she continued, "We all met for a cocktail in the lounge before dinner, as we did the previous evening. Stephanie commented on how beautiful my purse looked and asked to see it close up. She liked the diamonds. Since she was sitting across from me, it was too far to stretch. I passed it round the table for her to see. Marina and Alicia also held it and admired it. Then Stephanie passed it back round the table the other way so Laura could see it. Everybody at the table touched the purse. I really do think this is a ridiculous path you are going down, Mr. Manning."

"Perhaps." Richard was noncommittal. "Even so, I would like to borrow the pill box."

"Do you intend to check for poisonous powder?" she asked sarcastically.

"If I may just have it for a short while, I needn't trouble you any further."

"I trust that is a truly sincere remark, Mr. Manning." Marshall interjected."How do we know what you are going to do with the box? For all any of us know, you could have been the culprit. None of us knows anything about you or what brought you on this cruise."

Richard ignored the remark.

"I must insist on getting the box back," Sylvia said firmly.

"Of course. I do thank you for your time, Mrs. Sinclair. Once again, my condolences to you."

No sooner had he left the cabin, than Marshall quizzed Sylvia. "Why on earth did you let him take that pill box?"

Sylvia was startled. "Well, why ever not? It's no big deal. Besides, they haven't even established yet that Brian was murdered. He would have told us if they had."

"Even so, there was no need for you to put ideas into his head."

"Oh, Marshall. Don't be so silly. You're over-reacting."

"There is something about that man I don't like. I don't trust him for a minute. I just wonder what the hell he is up to."

Even Sylvia was now a little suspicious of the mysterious man.

Outside the door, Richard wrapped the pill box in a tissue from his pocket, and listened closely to the voices inside the cabin. He turned quickly as he heard a door open next to him. Stephanie emerged.

"You haven't been troubling my mother any further, have you Mr. Manning?" She was still annoyed with him.

"I just took a few minutes of her time, I can assure you."

"Well, I'll see if she views your visit the same way. Good day, Mr. Manning." She swept passed him and knocked on the door of her mother's cabin. "Mother, it's me. Stephanie," she called through the door.

Richard continued along the corridor, climbed the stairs onto the deck, and made his way to the parade of shops. The Harrods department store was a smallish boutique and was quite empty when he entered. He wandered around noting the quality merchandise, and not to his surprise, he found what he was seeking. There, on the counter was a small display of pill boxes, adorned with the same motif as the one in his pocket.

"May I help you, Sir?" inquired the shop assistant in her musical cockney accent.

Richard observed the pretty young saleslady. How English she looked, as he noted her pale face, pink cheeks, and soft blue eyes. She couldn't have been more than twenty years old, and looked quite innocent. She was sporting a very plain cream colored frock which bore a name tag "Celia" in the green and gold Harrods colors.

"I am hoping you can, Celia. That is, if you don't mind me calling you Celia?"

"Not at all, Sir."

"Do you know if you sold any of these pillboxes yesterday?" Richard pointed to the little display rack.

"Sir?" Celia was confused by the unusual request.

"I was just wondering if you sold any of these boxes yesterday."

"Well it's a pretty popular seller, if that's what you're asking. It sells when we have a lot of turbulence on the ship. That's when people get sea sick and they come in here for the boxes. The sales soar when that happens." She laughed slightly nervously, wondering what this gentleman wanted from her.

"I'm sure they do. But I am specifically interested in yesterday."

"Why yesterday, Sir?" Celia was baffled.

Richard opened his wallet, pulled out a five pound note, and handed it to her.

"Oh, I couldn't accept that, Sir. I'd get into trouble."

"It will be our secret." He winked at her, as he pressed the money into her hand.

Celia pocketed the money, slightly embarrassed and feeling guilty.

"Actually, I wouldn't really know as I wasn't on duty yesterday, although it does look as if we sold one, Sir."

"Oh? How do you know that?" He was skeptical.

"Well, there are only five on the rack. If you notice

the rack has room to hold six. At the end of the day, we're supposed to replenish all the racks of merchandise so they're ready for the next day. I guess Gretchen forgot to fill the rack."

"Who's Gretchen?"

"Gretchen Kingsley. She's the other lady that works here. It's her day off today."

"Could the pillbox have been sold this morning?"

"No Sir. I opened the shop this morning, and I've been the only one on duty. Unless someone stole one while I wasn't looking," she said impishly.

"How can I get in touch with Gretchen?"

"Well, she rooms with me. But I couldn't possibly give you our cabin number."

Richard reached into his wallet and showed her another five pound note. "I'm sure you have a phone in your cabin to communicate when necessary. Please see if you can get her on the telephone?"

"What's all this about, anyway?" Celia asked.

Richard pushed the money into her hand for a second time. "Could you please just dial the number?" She started dialing.

"Gretchen? Did you happen to sell one of those pill boxes yesterday?" She paused for a reply. "Well, you see, you forgot to fill up the rack when you left."

"Could you just pass me the telephone please?" Richard said impatiently, extending his hand.

"Hold on, Gretchen. There's a gentleman here who wants to ask you some questions about the sale." Celia passed the phone to Richard.

"Good day, Miss Kingsley. The name is Manning. Richard Manning. I would like to know if you can remember who purchased the pillbox yesterday? Was it a male or a female?"

Celia busied herself at the counter. She could hear Richard's side of the conversation and was intrigued by all the interest in a pill box.

"I see ... Are you sure of that? ... Miss Kingsley, are you one hundred percent positive ? ... No, no, indeed you have been most helpful. Thank you for your time, and have a nice day." He passed the receiver back to Celia.

He patted her gently on the hand. "Thank you so much for your help. You have a wonderful shop here."

"Please come back, Sir," she called after him as he hastened out of the store. She was still mystified by all the fuss over a pill box.

Richard looked at his watch, and with the time difference to the mainland, tried to figure out how late it was. Before going to the captain, he needed to make a couple of telephone calls.

CHAPTER 27

Richard entered the captain's office anxious to learn news of the Doctor's report.

"What did Doctor Raymond have for us?"

"Well, here is his report. He confirmed that poison was found in the body. In short, he found very substantial traces of ricin."

"Very, very interesting, Captain. Ricin can come in the form of powder or a pill. That is most, most helpful, though not altogether unsuspected."

"Oh, why is that? You must have discovered something of significance in the meantime?"

"Well, how much do you know about Maurizio?"

"Maurizio DiCaponi? What has he got to do with this?" The Captain was totally perplexed.

"How long has he worked for you?"

"Well, this is his first trip. I don't understand the connection." He was still baffled.

"Isn't it unusual for a new employee to be placed in such a position? I mean working in the top restaurant and serving the star 'guests of honor'?"

"I suppose so. We usually promote from within. But Maurizio has impeccable credentials. He worked at the Hotel Danieli in Venice. As you must be aware, the Danieli is one of *the* hotels in Europe. He worked with our Maitre D', who was employed there a few years ago. Frankly, he was more qualified than any of the stewards we currently have in any of our restaurants."

"Did he apply to you for the position or did your Maitre D' reach out to him?"

"I'm not too sure about that. We'd have to find out from him. He handles all the hirings and firings in that department. When we have staff meetings I'm just notified as a matter of professional courtesy. Occasionally, I'll question things, but typically, I leave employment matters to my department heads. Alex has never given me cause for concern."

"Alex? Who is Alex?"

"Alex Vescari. He is our Maitre D'. The best in the business, I believe. He has always overseen all our restaurants in a most exemplary manner."

"Is it possible for us to have a chat with him?"

"What? Regarding Maurizio?" The captain shook his head. "I do think you are way off the mark on this one, Richard. I still don't see the connection."

"Then please humor me, Captain."

The captain paused for a while then sighed. "All right. Let's see what we can do." He pressed the intercom to his assistant outside. "Please see if you can locate Alex Vescari, and ask him to report to me here as soon as possible, will you?"

"Right away, Sir," replied the efficient voice at the other end of the intercom.

Within minutes, Alex Vescari entered the office. He was in his mid thirties with jet black wavy hair, dark eyes, and olive complexion. "You wanted to see me, Sir?" he asked in his slight accent.

He must be quite a ladies man, Richard thought, noticing how striking he appeared in his uniform.

"Yes. Thank you for coming. This is Mr. Richard Manning." The two gentlemen shook hands. "You may or may not be aware that we had a death on this ship last evening."

"I heard, Captain. Mr. Sinclair, I believe."

"Correct. Mr. Manning is a private investigator, and is assisting me with the investigation."

"Investigation, Sir? What investigation?"

"Confidentially, Alex, it seems that Brian Sinclair was murdered."

"Murdered, Sir? By whom? And why?"

"We're not sure. Richard Manning wanted to ask you a few questions about Maurizio."

"Maurizio?" Alex was stunned. "You're not accusing Maurizio of murder? That's impossible."

"No," the captain reassured him. "We are not accusing Maurizio of murder. Mr. Manning just has a few questions."

Richard took over the conversation. "How long have you known Maurizio?"

"I've known him since he was a teenager. He was hired at the Hotel Danieli almost ten years ago as a dishwasher and worked his way up. I trained him. He is one of the most loyal, hardworking and trustworthy individuals I have ever known."

"So you were close friends then?"

"Oh, no! I wouldn't say close friends. He was a loner. Ours was more a professional relationship. We respected each other. But after I left, we would always get together for a drink and maybe dinner whenever I was in Venice. It is my home town after all. I have family there."

"How did he come to work on board this ship? Did you approach him or did he approach you?"

"No, he contacted me a couple of months ago."

"Did he say why?"

Alex shrugged. "He said he needed a change. He was tired of the Hotel Danieli. Thought he would like to travel and to see a bit of the world. Said it would be nice to work with me again. We had a vacancy, and I jumped at the chance to hire him."

"Did he ever have any girlfriends?"

"I'm sure he did. He is a very handsome young man. They were always after him at the hotel. The young ladies would — how do you say it? — 'swoon' over him."

Richard smiled. "I'm sure. But, to your knowledge, did he ever have one special girlfriend that he mentioned to you?"

Alex shook his head as he considered the question. "Not that I am aware of. But then, as I said, when we met, we talked about the hotel, people we knew there, people we liked, people we didn't like. I would ask about certain members of the staff, and he would tell me if they had left or if they were still there. I would ask about some of the hotel guests who would return on a regular basis. We would always have lots of laughs over them." He chuckled as he recalled the conversations in his mind.

"How about his family? Did he ever talk about his family?"

The captain was getting tired of what he considered an exercise in futility. He interrupted. "Richard, I think I have indulged your humor quite enough. Alex does have work to do today. Is there anything that you have to ask that may be pertinent?"

"Sorry, Captain. You're quite right. Thank you for your indulgence. I just have one more question for Mr. Vescari."

"What is that, Mr. Manning?"

"How was it that Maurizio DiCaponi was assigned to the Sinclair table?"

Alex shrugged again. "I don't exactly recall the specifics. When we were interviewing him, reviewing salary, work schedule and everything, I think he mentioned that he would have to have the best seating assignments if he accepted the position, and be serving the important guests. He said it more as a joke though. I told him that with his experience he was more highly qualified than our existing staff, and that, of course, he would be given senior ranking and assignments."

"How did the other staff take that?"

Alex was indignant. "My personnel do not question my decisions nor my authority, Sir."

The captain was anxious not to have his Maitre D' upset. "Thank you for your time, Alex. You may resume your duties."

"Thank you, Sir." He nodded toward the captain, shook Richard's hand, and moved toward the door before turning around.

"If you are accusing Maurizio of murder, I am certain he didn't do it."

"Pray tell, why is that?" Richard was curious to hear his answer.

"What possible motive could he have? I do not believe he knew Mr. Sinclair."

"Indeed. Thank you, Mr. Vescari. Your information has been most insightful, as well as helpful."

Alex closed the door behind himself.

The captain approached Richard. "I would have to agree with Alex, Richard. What possible motive could Maurizio have for murdering Brian Sinclair?"

"Who is accusing Maurizio of murder?"

"Then what was the purpose of all this? Smacks to me of a red herring."

"Not at all, Captain. I believe Maurizio is the very key to the whole mystery."

"I am not following this at all. Would you care to elaborate?"

"Why don't you page Maurizio, and I believe it will all become clear?"

"If I contact Maurizio, it will be against my better judgment."

"And if you don't, Captain, we may never solve this mystery for sure."

The captain twiddled his thumbs for a few moments then pressed the button on his intercom.

"Yes, Sir," came the response.

"Could you please have Maurizio DiCaponi report to my office as soon as possible?"

CHAPTER 28

Maurizio appeared calm and controlled as he seated himself, yet Richard knew that he had to be both curious and suspicious. He decided to take a calculated gamble.

"Mr. DiCaponi, when we dock at New York harbor you will immediately be placed under arrest and taken into the custody of the New York police," he announced assertively.

"What?" exclaimed Maurizio, aghast. He leapt to his feet. The captain also jumped out of his chair.

"Mr. Manning, this is an outrage. You will retract that statement," the captain demanded, furious at such an accusation against one of his staff members.

Richard was determined and confidant. "I will not make any such retraction. I have plenty of evidence to prove that Maurizio DiCaponi is indeed the murderer of Mr. Brian Sinclair."

"This is ridiculous. I'm not staying to listen to such wild accusations," Maurizio said contemptuously, as he turned and headed toward the door.

"My accusations are neither wild nor ridiculous. Captain, you must order Mr. DiCaponi to remain," Richard insisted. "He is perfectly free to refute anything I have to say."

"Maurizio, please sit back down. I would like to hear

what Richard Manning has to say, and then you can feel free to address any of the charges."

Maurizio paused and slowly returned to his chair. The captain continued. "I'm warning you, your case had better be good, Mr. Manning," choosing the formal method of addressing the private investigator as if to underscore the severity of the situation. "This is a very serious charge. I will not tolerate any falsehoods against any members of my crew. Indeed, charges may well be filed against you, should your accusations prove to be unfounded."

"Fair enough, Captain. That seems reasonable," Richard acknowledged. Maurizio shifted uncomfortably in his seat, his elbow on the side of the chair and his chin resting in his hand.

"We started our investigation, Captain, with a false premise," Richard began, as he paced the floor, hands clasped behind his back. "We naturally assumed that Mr. Sinclair's drink had been poisoned while he was at the dance table, and that it was one of the guests who placed something in the glass. It was unfortunate we had to wait so long for the good doctor to inform us what the poison was. We now know that the poison was ricin, which can remain in the body for quite a while before taking effect. As you know, Captain, not one of the guests was without suspicion or without cause. Indeed, every one of the guests had the motive and the opportunity. But as we were leaving Stephanie and Jean-Louis' cabin, I noticed a small Harrods shopping bag. I recalled our earlier conversation with David and Laura Clayton. Mrs. Clayton, in a feeble attempt to deflect suspicion from herself and her husband, told us of a pill box that Mrs. Sinclair had purchased at

Harrods whilst she was in London. Naturally, I dismissed the notion at the time. After we left Stephanie's cabin, I visited Mrs. Sinclair and asked for the pill box, which I currently have in my possession. I understand that last night, when Mrs. Sinclair retrieved the pill box from her handbag, you, Maurizio, had it placed on your tray, which you then carried to the other end of the table to Mr. Sinclair."

Maurizio squirmed uneasily. He felt the sweat on the palms of his hands. "But that is all I did," he countered. "Mrs. Sinclair placed the box on the tray. I did not touch it."

"Ah, but I think you did Mr. DiCaponi. During that time, I believe you retrieved a replica containing the poisonous ricin from your pocket, and switched it with the pill box on the tray. Naturally, before returning to the other end of the table, you did not have the time to empty out the pill from Mrs. Sinclair's box, though you certainly might have tried."

"This is absolutely ridiculous," interjected Maurizio testily.

"Is it?" inquired Richard, as he stared directly at Maurizio. "I don't think so. As steward assigned to the table, you were in a position to overhear the conversation regarding the Harrods pill box the previous evening."

"I'm not sure where all this is headed. Could you please get to the point?" the captain inquired.

"Of course, my dear fellow. Apparently, Mrs. Sinclair announced that she had purchased the box at Harrods, and that it was probably available at the shop on board. I visited the Harrods store earlier today, after I had seen Mrs. Sinclair. The shop assistant was most cordial and confirmed that only one of the particular pill boxes carrying the same motif as Mrs. Sinclair's had been sold since the ship set sail. The records indicate that you, Mr. DiCaponi, were the one who made the sole purchase."

Maurizio was even more agitated. He shifted in his chair from one side to the other. "So what? There is no law against purchasing a box for my pills is there? In any event, what possible motive could I have? Until Monday evening, I had never even met Mr. Sinclair."

"Maurizio does have a point, Richard," noted the baffled captain.

"Yes, that had me fooled for a while too," Richard continued. "I contacted my connections on the mainland. I can assure you, I have many very credible sources in the United States, the British Police, and Interpol."

Maurizio turned to the captain. "Sir, may I please leave so I can continue my duties? I do not see that I should subject myself to the innuendos of this two-bit investigator."

Before the captain could respond, Richard placed his hands on Maurizio's chair, locking him in. "Your real name is not DiCaponi, is it?"

"Get away from me, Mr. Manning, or whatever your name is."

"Is it?" Richard asked again more firmly, glaring down at his suspect. Maurizio remained silent, his eyes fixated on his inquisitor. Beads of sweat were beginning to form on his brow.

Richard stepped back. He was like a lion going for the kill.

"I put it to you that DiCaponi was the name of your stepfather — the man who married your mother. You are, in fact, the son of Terri and Greg Calderman. Greg Calderman, the very man who was in partnership with Brian Sinclair and who committed suicide. Yet, your mother and certain others believe that Brian Sinclair was responsible for your father's death. Isn't that true, Mr. Calderman?" Richard raised his voice a notch louder and became more aggressive.

"What nonsense! Captain, I must insist you intervene and stop this harassment."

"You came here to avenge your father's death, didn't you?" Maurizio looked at Richard, his face filled with disdain. "Isn't that true, Mr. Calderman?" Richard was almost shouting, as he leaned closer, staring directly into Maurizio's face. "I am sure your fingerprints can be found on the pill box that I have in my possession, Mr. Maurizio Calderman."

"This is ridiculous. Mr. Sinclair died at the table near the dance floor. I was nowhere near when he died."

"But Mr. Sinclair was killed with ricin. Ricin does not cause an instantaneous death. You knew they would all be going to the dance after dinner, where Mr. Sinclair was surrounded by friends and family. Sufficient time would have lapsed. You *did* kill Mr. Sinclair, didn't you?"

Maurizio suddenly leapt to his feet and angrily shot back. "Damn right I killed that son of a bitch! My mother told me stories about what a great man my father was. Do you know what it is like to grow up without a father? No. Of course you don't." He looked at both Richard and the captain, the tone of his voice becoming one of derision.

"Do you know what it is like to grow up in poverty in a country where you can't even speak the language? My mother had nothing when she arrived in Napoli. She could not get work. She did menial house cleaning, scrubbing floors while trying to keep me clothed and fed. It was degrading." He looked back and forth between both men. "She met and married an Italian, who had charmed her and who promised to adopt me. I thought I would finally have a father who loved me. But he was a drunk and possessive. He would beat my mother. There was nothing I could do, and I would go to sleep at night with the pillow covering my head so I would not have to hear it. One night we left Napoli, again with nothing, and fled to Venezia. My mother got a job making beds at the Hotel Danieli. As soon as I was old enough, I was able to get work in the kitchen washing the dishes so I could help pay the bills. My mother deserved a better life — and so did I." He paused. Silence fell in the room.

"How did you know Mr. Sinclair would be aboard this ship?" asked the captain. It was something that puzzled Richard Manning too.

"I was resting at home one night late, watching television. There is a program that comes from America. It is called 'America Sings'. Occasionally, I watch it. This night, one of the guest panelists was Brian Sinclair. It was the first time I had ever set eyes on the man. He said that he and his wife were celebrating their 25th wedding anniversary by taking the QEII luxury liner from Southampton to New York. He was so conceited and cocky. Clearly he had everything — half of which should have been my father's. The next day I contacted my good friend Alex Vescari to see about getting a job aboard the ship. I started planning the way to get rid of Brian Sinclair then and there," he continued, his voice filled with contempt. "My girlfriend at the time worked in a pharmacy. She'd do anything for me. It was simple for her to obtain the ricin. One has to be very careful with it. We wore gloves as we mixed the ricin with aspirin powder and put it into an empty capsule. I was ready. I didn't know how I would accomplish the act once on board, but I knew I would figure out a way. It all became simple once I overheard Mrs. Clayton comment on the pill box, and Mrs. Sinclair saying she could probably purchase one at the Harrods store on the ship. The fact that Mr. Sinclair had to have a blood pressure pill every night, made it even simpler. You're right, Mr. Manning. I did try to switch the boxes back, but I could not open Mrs. Sinclair's box. The little locket was jammed. I had to keep her box."

"You realize that you will be confined to your quarters for the duration of the trip," the captain noted in a matter of fact tone. Maurizio nodded.

"But, you know what, Captain? I do not regret what I did for one moment."

Richard intervened. "You may not wish to say anything further, until you have an attorney present, Mr. Calderman."

"I don't care, Mr. Manning. If I have to spend the rest of my life in jail, Brian Sinclair will be rotting in hell."

Not for the first time, the room fell silent. Richard was quietly pleased with himself. The captain was annoyed that Richard had not taken him into his confidence. Maurizio sat with his hands clasped together and his head down.

"Do you wish to inform Mrs. Sinclair or shall I?" Richard asked the captain.

"I think we should both see her."

He pressed his intercom.

"Yes, Sir," came the voice at the other end.

"Could you please have security report to me immediately?"

"Yes, Captain."

"I'll need two officers to escort Maurizio DiCaponi to his cabin."

"Right away, Captain."

Maurizio buried his head in his hands and began to cry.

CHAPTER 29

T he only sound that could be heard at the dinner table that evening was that of ice cubes rattling as Todd toyed with his near empty glass of scotch. Everyone sat uneasily in their assigned seats, eyeing their host and hostess's empty chairs.

"Well, is it safe to assume that my contract can be completed now, Marshall?"

Marshall was stunned at the insensitivity and timing of Todd's question. "Actually, I think it is probably a little premature at this stage," he sidestepped. But before he could elaborate, Robin interceded.

"I think all business matters really need to be addressed through me, since I am probably now the major stockholder."

"Oh, knock it off, Robin. Is that all you care about?" Stephanie snapped harshly.

"You knock it off, Sis. Just because you are probably no longer a beneficiary is no reason to snap at me," he retorted.

"I'm just tired of your pompous and arrogant attitude."

Marina attempted to defuse the mounting argument. "Maybe, we all need to just step back a little. Everyone is distraught right now. We should be focusing on the well-being of Sylvia at this time, don't you think?" She looked at the siblings for reaction.

"You're totally right, my dear, of course," Todd

acknowledged. "Forgive me all, for my insensitivity." He looked around in vain for the waiter. "I wonder what one has to do around here to get a drink. I could certainly use another scotch."

"What else is new?" mumbled Laura to herself, heard only by David who gave her a disapproving look as he kicked her gently under the table. He picked up the thread of Marina's comments and continuing to address Stephanie and Robin, "Certainly, you both know that we are all here for you and your mother, if you need us for anything. Hopefully, that goes without saying."

Stephanie smiled. "Thanks, David. I appreciate it, and I know Mother does."

"How is Sylvia holding up?" inquired Laura. "We tried to call her a few times, and went and knocked on the door, but there was no reply."

"She called me earlier and spoke to Jean-Louis," Stephanie responded. "She told him her telephone was switched off. The doctor had given her a sedative which would help her get some sleep, or at least, some rest."

Jill chimed in. "Well, I just wonder what Sylvia is going to do when she gets back to that mansion. I mean, gee, it is so huge. Can you imagine rattling around in that big house all by yourself? I think she should sell it. Maybe just get a smaller home."

"Why, thank you, Jill. I will pass your sage advice onto my mother," Stephanie responded caustically. "I am sure she will consider your opinion and knowledge invaluable." *I wish someone would just throw the tramp overboard*, she thought.

"I still can't believe Maurizio did it," said Alicia,

changing the subject. She was full of mixed emotions. She wished she had studied Maurizio's face and habits more and been less dismissive of him. After all, he was the son of the true love of her life. She was secretly pleased in a way that Greg Calderman's death had been avenged — if indeed Greg was murdered as Denise had said. She was very confused.

"Well, he's obviously just psycho, that's all," shrugged Todd.

"Not necessarily, dear," Marina chided her husband. "None of us know the road he has travelled, nor do we know any of the actual details. Frankly, it all seems rather sketchy to me."

Todd blew Marina a kiss across the table. "That's my wife, always the understanding one," his voice laced with sarcasm. But then his demeanor turned. "The damn waiter just killed the husband of your best friend, and you're defending him? He's a murderer. Do you get it? A murderer. What the hell's the matter with you, woman?" He glared at her.

Marina was embarrassed and humiliated. She wrapped her shawl around her shoulders. "There is no need to shout at me. All I was saying was ..."

Todd did not allow her to finish. "We all know what you were saying, Marina. Who cares about the damn circumstances? Bottom line is he killed Brian — husband, father, and friend to all of us around this table." He picked up his glass and drained the remnants of his diluted scotch.

Jean-Louis had said nothing up to this point. "I agree with you, Todd. Even though everyone here knows that

Brian and I did not see eye to eye — we never did, and probably never would — but he did not deserve to die. I don't care about the details, Marina. My grandchild will grow up without a grandfather. Nothing will ever be able to change that — and no amount of justification or Maurizio's reasoning will satisfy me, nor ,would I imagine, my wife. However, you are right about one thing, Marina. Now is not the time for anger, or for yelling at each other." He reached out across the table for Stephanie's hand and started to stroke it gently. "Stephanie is already enduring enough stress and trauma, which she does not need in her condition."

"Stephanie is not the only one who happens to be suffering, you know," Robin retorted mockingly. "She is not the only one dealing with 'stress and trauma'."

Jean-Louis shot back aggressively. "I know that, Robin. But Stephanie happens to be my wife, and since she is pregnant, neither of us wants anything to happen to the baby."

"It's not the second coming," Robin commented coldly.

"All right, I've had enough," Marshall thundered. "All this petty bickering is not getting any of us anywhere. We are all in a state of shock over Brian's death. Maybe we don't know the cause or reason for it. But what I do know is this." He pointed his finger toward the cabins, "There is also a woman in one of those cabins who is also a friend, mother and wife, or should I say, widow, now?" He paused for effect. "If anyone is going through pain and suffering, it is Sylvia. She is the one who will be facing the future alone."

"Not as long as you're around," quipped Robin acerbically.

"I'll ignore that disgusting remark for now, Robin." Then, returning to his thought process, continued. "Does anyone here think that if Sylvia were here tonight, she would be happy with all this petulant sniping? Everyone at each others' throats? Does anyone even care about how Sylvia would feel if she were a witness to the conversation thus far this evening?"

"Bravo. I couldn't agree with you more, Marshall," David noted.

Laura sided with her husband. "Yes. In fact, if there is any more unpleasantness this evening, I think maybe David and I will just have dinner in our cabins. We just thought that all of us being here together this evening might ease the grief. That's the only reason we came tonight, and to show our support for Sylvia."

Todd started thinking about his contract. "You're right, Marshall. I've been behaving like a jackass. Sorry, everyone." Marina heaved a sigh of relief.

"Well then, since everyone wants a *kumbaya* moment, let's change the subject. What shall we all talk about?" Robin asked. He was feeling bellicose that evening.

"I know," squeaked Jill. "Let's think of babies names for Stephanie and Jean-Louis. If it's a girl maybe you could name her Jill," she giggled.

At that moment, the new steward appeared at the dinner table. "My apologies, ladies and gentlemen. There has been a slight change in staff assignments. My name is Alex Vescari. I will be tending your needs for the duration of the cruise. I will bring this evening's dinner menus shortly. Can I interest anyone in a cocktail?"

"Scotch on the rocks. Make that a double," Todd called out, as everyone else shook their heads.

"I will be right back with your cocktail, Sir, and menus for everyone. Thank you for your patience." He departed.

Jill picked up where she left off. "Well he's certainly a hunk. Maybe we ladies could discuss him, before the babies' names. I know. If it's a boy, you could name him Alex after our new waiter." She continued chuckling.

Robin was exasperated. "Jill, can you please keep quiet with your thoughts and just focus on the menu and what you want to eat for dinner tonight? You would be doing us all a favor."

Jill looked downward and felt chastised. She was not about to confront Robin at the dinner table. She knew that mood, and hoped that someone would leap to her defense.

Unfortunately for her, no one did. It was the only comment from Robin that evening that all those gathered at the table happened to agree upon.

CHAPTER 30

It was early morning as Sylvia stood outside on the deck while the ship sailed slowly into New York harbor. It was cold, and she was wrapped in a dark fur coat and a headscarf. Despite the fact it was only just dawn, she sported a pair of fashionable dark glasses. It had been two days since Brian was murdered, and she was eager to return home to some solitude. Her anniversary had turned into the worst imaginable nightmare.

"There you are, Mother. We've been searching all over for you," Stephanie called out as she and Jean-Louis made their way hastily along the deck. "Jean-Louis said you'd be here."

Sylvia gave her a wan smile as they embraced. "I thought it would be nice to see the Statue of Liberty."

"I told you, Stephanie. Lady Liberty has a special place in the heart for all immigrants," smiled Jean-Louis as he kissed his mother-in-law on both cheeks.

"Please let me come and stay with you, Mother. I could easily change my flights," Stephanie pleaded.

"No, dear. I'll be fine, thank you. Marshall has promised to oversee the funeral arrangements. I'm sure he'll take care of whatever needs attending to. I just need to go home now."

"Well, maybe I can stay with you for a few days after Dad's funeral."

"Yes, that would be better. I'd like that. That is if Jean-Louis doesn't mind."

"Not at all. Maybe you can do some shopping together and buy some clothes for the baby," Jean-Louis offered, attempting to bring a joyful thought to the conversation.

There was a shriek from further down the deck. "Hey, there's your mother and Stephanie." It was Jill. *Heaven preserve us*, thought Sylvia, as Jill came running toward them, followed by Robin. "I guess it's the thing to get up early and come on deck to see the Statue," she burbled. "It's just a grey piece of concrete. Personally, I don't know what all the fuss is about."

"No I don't suppose you do," Sylvia commented drily as she hugged her son. She fervently hoped that this would be her last meeting with Jill Potts.

"You really don't get it, do you?" an irritated Stephanie asked.

"Get what?" Jill was confused and looked at Robin. Over his shoulder, she could see a flurry of activity farther along the deck, and strained to see what was happening. A few tourists were gravitating toward one of the passengers. "Oh, wow! It's that Denise Parker. Look! She's headed toward us."

"Sylvia, darling," Denise chirped, as she embraced Sylvia. "I'm so dreadfully sorry to hear about Brian. I'm just devastated, as I'm sure you must be."

Sylvia nodded. "Thank you, Denise."

"Maybe you can have dinner with me while you are in Manhattan."

"Actually, we're heading straight back to Los Angeles. There's much to arrange before the funeral."

"Ah, yes. Well at least you'll have your family. Are these your children?"

"Yes. This is my daughter, Stephanie, and her husband, Jean-Louis. And this is my son, Robin, and his girlfriend, Jill." Then gesturing with her hand, "Of course, you all know Denise Parker."

"Wow," repeated Jill. "Can I get your autograph, Miss Parker?" She fumbled in her pockets for a piece of paper and a pen, while popping a bubble with her chewing gum.

Denise looked at Jill with disdain, and turned to Sylvia. "You must be thrilled," she offered sarcastically, the observation lost on Jill.

"Ecstatic," Sylvia responded with equal sarcasm.

"Well, let me give you my card. Please call me next time you're in New York. Maybe we can do lunch or dinner."

Sylvia nodded, "Maybe."

Denise noticed Marshall heading toward them, with Laura and David. Not wanting to involve herself in conversation with any of them, she extricated herself.

"Well, it's been lovely seeing you after all this time, Sylvia." She hugged the woman to whom she had lost her fiancée many years earlier. "Once again, my sympathies to all of you on your loss. Brian really was such a wonderful man. Do keep in touch now. Goodbye, darlings."

Sylvia watched Denise as she headed further down the deck, wondering whether Denise was being sincere or if it was just a theatrical façade. It seemed a strange irony that Denise may have been the one person who probably understood what she was going through.

"What the hell did she want?" growled Marshall as he arrived.

"Oh, she just wanted to express her condolences," Sylvia said noncommittally. "I suppose she meant well."

"I still can't believe that young boy is responsible for Brian's death. I was astounded when I learned he was Greg's son," Laura exclaimed, hugging Sylvia.

"Who's Greg?" Jill asked.

Ignoring her, David recalled, "Well, actually there is some vague resemblance. Remember on the first night of the cruise, Brian even remarked he thought he'd seen the steward somewhere before? There's no way it would have occurred to him it was Greg's son.

"Who's Greg?" Jill asked again.

Robin was getting exasperated by Jill's behavior. "Jill, let it go." He grabbed her by the hand. "Come on, let's see if we can grab some coffee for everyone."

The ship's horn blew, just as the torch from the Statue of Liberty could be seen in the distance.

"Ah, just in time," said Todd, as he and Marina arrived on deck with Alicia. "Can't arrive in New York by ship without seeing Lady Liberty, can we?" They all hugged Sylvia, who pulled a tissue from her purse and wiped her eye.

"I can't thank you enough for all your support these last couple of days. It has meant so much to me." She was overcome.

Laura felt a pang of guilt as she moved forward to console the grieving widow. Marshall beat her to the post, and placed his comforting arm around Sylvia. "We'll be here for you — always."

The party was distracted as the Statue of Liberty loomed closer, and they all discussed its significance.

Finally, the ship docked at the harbor, and the group prepared for the interminable clearing of customs.

From her vantage point, Sylvia could see Maurizio being escorted down the gangplank by the security officers. No one else seemed to notice. Even though her heart was filled with rage, she decided that it would be better to keep quiet.

The captain arrived. "I saw your son and his girlfriend in the coffee lounge, Mrs Sinclair. They told me you were here. Once again, I wanted to convey my condolences. I have arranged with the customs and immigration for you to proceed through a special line. I will be more than happy to escort you."

"You have been most kind, Captain." They started to move to the gangway. "Please be sure and thank Richard Manning for me, won't you? I do have his card. I'll write to him when I get back to Los Angeles."

"I'm sure he'll appreciate that, Mrs. Sinclair." He gestured to the customs official.

Sylvia extended her hand as she turned to face him. "Goodbye, Captain. Thank you for everything."

He removed his hat, and shook her hand. "Goodbye, Mrs Sinclair. I do hope we meet again under more favorable circumstances."

She smiled feebly, as she headed toward the immigration counter.

"Welcome home," the official stated, as he reviewed her documents.

Home indeed, she thought, as she pondered her future without Brian. As much as she disliked being alone, the thought of solitude somehow helped her grief.

She slept most of the flight back to Los Angeles, and was comforted to be met by Jack, the chauffeur from Sinclair Records. *How sweet of Marshall to arrange that for me*, she thought.

The car pulled into the driveway at her mansion. Helen, her loyal maid and housekeeper, was there to greet her.

"I am so very sorry to hear about Mr. Sinclair, Ma'am," she said greeting her employer with a hug.

"Thank you, Helen," Sylvia responded, and climbed wearily up the steps into the house. Jack followed with the luggage. It was late afternoon and the sun was beginning to set.

"Would you like some dinner or a snack?" asked Helen.

Sylvia glanced at her watch and thought for a moment. "No thank you, Helen. I think before going upstairs, I'll just have a sherry on the front porch." She poured herself a drink, and moved slowly outside. Listening to the hum of the traffic on the nearby streets, she sat down and surveyed the mountains and the garden.

There would be no more waiting for Brian to return from the office and join her for a drink each night. She sipped her sherry and allowed the tears to flow down her cheeks.

The ringing of the telephone startled her, almost causing the sherry to spill on her lap. She wiped her eyes, placed the glass on the table, and made her way to the telephone.

"I'll get it, Helen," she called out, while removing one

of her earrings. It was a relief to hear Marshall's voice at the other end of the line.

"Just wanted to check that you got back safely," he said.

"That's very sweet and thoughtful of you, Marshall. You really are an angel. I am probably going to be relying on you more heavily in the future."

"I'll always be here for you, Sylvia. You know that, don't you?"

"I know. You've been a loyal friend to both Brian and me all these years. Don't think it hasn't been appreciated." Sylvia had always known that Marshall was in love with her, and had hoped that as time went by and Marshall saw how much she loved Brian, his feelings would change. She sensed they hadn't, but there was nothing she could do to alter that. To her, he would always be a close family friend.

"I'll be back in Los Angeles tomorrow. Is there anything I can do in the meantime?"

"Thank you, I'm fine."

"No, really. How are you Sylvia?"

"I truly am ok. But I can't stop thinking about Maurizio's motives for killing Brian. I can't believe he would think Brian could have had Greg Calderman murdered. It was widely known and well-publicized that he committed suicide. He was caught red-handed with his hand in the till."

"Well, I'm certainly not defending Maurizio. But, who knows what thoughts Terri put into his head when he was growing up in Italy? Who knows how unbalanced he might be?"

"I suppose you're right. Anyone who knows Brian though, must surely know he would be incapable of such a thing."

"Try not to think about it too much, Sylvia. Try and get a good night's sleep."

She ignored his comments. "The next thing I will have to deal with is the will. Don't know why, but I'm just dreading it."

"It's really not that complex, Sylvia. Brian, as you know had two final wills. One he signed, and the other is unsigned. In both, he left the house and everything outside the business to you. There are a couple of minor provisions for people like Helen, whom he has left a couple of thousand dollars. You're the majority shareholder in Sinclair records. He left me a very small percentage. The only difference in the wills is that in the one, he left Robin twenty percent of the shares and nothing for Stephanie. In the other, he left them ten percent each. The wills are in the safe. You know the combination, you can find out for yourself."

"I might just do that, Marshall. Thanks for the heads up."

They hung up, and Sylvia returned to finish her sherry. She sat in quiet contemplation for a short while, and then curiosity got the better of her. She finished her drink, headed to the office, and unlocked the safe to retrieve both wills. She was relieved to see that the one Brian had signed, split the shares evenly between Robin and Stephanie. *Thank God*, she thought. *Robin will be ticked for a while, but he'll get over it.* She was pleased to read that if Marshall, Robin or Stephanie wanted to sell the shares, she would have first option. *You did well, Brian. You did well.* She smiled, as she closed the files and put them back in the safe.

"Good night, Helen," she called as she headed up the staircase to the bedroom.

"Good night ma'am."

Sylvia undressed and climbed into her bed. She looked at the moon shining through the window, and wondered how she would cope with being CEO of Sinclair Records and the legacy Brian had left behind.

ABOUT THE AUTHOR

Stephen Murray was born in England and raised in different countries throughout Southern Africa. Upon completion of his education, he returned to England before moving to California in 1976. He has traveled extensively throughout the world visiting all continents. Stephen owns a computer software company. Apart from traveling and writing, he enjoys theatre, concerts, music, reading and current affairs. Stephen is the author of two previously published novels — the award winning *The Chapel of Eternal Love* and its sequel *Return to the Chapel of Eternal Love*. He makes his home in Las Vegas, Nevada, where he has lived since May 2003.

For questions, comments or
to order additional copies of this book,
please visit www.authorstephenmurray.com
or email him at stephen@casandras.net.

Made in the USA
Las Vegas, NV
09 February 2023

67220189R00138